Heartland™
Out of the Darkness

Lauren Brooke

SCHOLASTIC

With special thanks to Gill Harvey

For Natacha — a good friend of Heartland

Scholastic Children's Books,
Euston House, 24 Eversholt Street,
London NW1 1DB, UK
a division of Scholastic Ltd
London ~ New York ~ Toronto ~ Sydney ~ Auckland
Mexico City ~ New Delhi ~ Hong Kong

Published in the UK by Scholastic Ltd, 2001
Series created by Working Partners Ltd

Copyright © Working Partners Ltd, 2001

Heartland is a trademark of Working Partners Ltd

10 digit ISBN 0 439 99436 5
13 digit ISBN 978 0439 99436 1

Typeset by TW Typesetting, Midsomer Norton, Somerset
Printed and bound by Nørhaven Paperback A/S, Viborg, Denmark

10

The right of Lauren Brooke to be identified as the author of this work has been asserted
by her in accordance with the Copyright, Designs and Patents Act, 1988.

Heartland ™

Out of the Darkness

Amy ran to the barn where she could already hear Prince stumbling around his stall. Just as she was about to draw back the bolt, there was a crack of thunder and the lighting cut out. The stalls were plunged into darkness.

Amy gasped. Suddenly she heard a frantic whinny. Gallant Prince! In the last, fading shreds of daylight, she saw the rolling whites of the stallion's eyes and the flash of his hooves as he reared up. He crashed down with his forelegs against the door of the stall, and reared again, letting out another high-pitched whinny. As his forelegs smashed into the door again, Amy heard the sound of splintering wood...

Other books in the series

Coming Home
After the Storm
Breaking Free
Taking Chances
Come What May
One Day You'll Know

Coming soon

Thicker Than Water

Chapter One

Sunlight glinted in the late-January afternoon, catching golden flecks in the filly's chestnut coat. Her nostrils quivered as she stared into the distance, detecting a scent on the breeze. Then, with a toss of her head, she wheeled in the snow and cantered towards her mother. Ducking under the mare's body, she began to suckle hungrily.

Amy watched from the gateway, reading every movement. The filly brought her head back up and nosed her mother's side, her bright eyes alert and curious.

"Here, Daybreak!" Amy called. Daybreak's head rose, listening. She stood still for an instant, then she took a few steps forward.

"That's it. Over here," Amy encouraged. Daybreak broke into a trot, and approached the gateway. Amy felt her heart leap as the filly reached for her, snorting eagerly and butting

Amy's arm with her velvety muzzle. Amy laid her hand on the filly's soft neck.

"Who'd have thought it?" said Ty, coming to stand at Amy's side. "She's so different."

"Isn't she?" Amy smiled happily.

Ty was eighteen, three years older than Amy, and the only other person at Heartland who knew as much about the horses as she did. He knew exactly how difficult Daybreak had been – until Christmas the filly hadn't trusted humans at all; not because she had been badly treated, but because she was born with an independent, fighting spirit. Now she was approaching Amy of her own free will.

Ty held out his hand for Daybreak to smell. She nudged it, gently blowing through her nostrils. "There's a girl," he murmured.

"She wouldn't have let you do that a week ago," Amy said. After nursing the filly back to health from a virus, Amy had finally bonded with her. Then she had made sure that Ty and Ben, the rest of the Heartland team, spent as much time as they could with the filly.

"She's definitely getting used to people now," Ty agreed. "You know, I think she's almost ready to go. We should start thinking about a new home for her and Melody soon."

"But she's only just over her virus, Ty," Amy protested. "And there's a whole load more handling work we need to do with her."

"Look at her, Amy," Ty said gently, as Daybreak stretched

out her nose, reaching to nibble the sleeve of his coat. "She's fully recovered. And she's not just accepting people now, she's actually *interested* in them, too."

Amy felt torn. There was something in what Ty was saying, but her bond with the foal still seemed so new and fragile. She didn't want to let her go – not yet.

"It's still early days, Ty," she said. "She might be interested in people, but that's just the start. We have to be sure of her before we let her go to someone else."

Ty shrugged and turned away and Amy suddenly felt uncomfortable. Gazing into the distance, she watched as a crow landed on the far side of the paddock. Daybreak saw it too, and broke away from them. As she cantered after the bird, she gave a high-spirited squeal.

"See?" Amy pointed out, feeling reassured. "She's still unpredictable."

Ty frowned thoughtfully. "Come on, Amy. She's just full of energy, and you know it. And anyway, the right owner would keep her on track. We can't keep Melody and Daybreak, it's against our rules. Besides, we need the stable for other horses – horses that really need our help."

Amy nodded. It was true. That was the way they worked – the way her mother had set up Heartland twelve years ago. Once horses had been treated successfully, they were always rehomed to make room for others.

"I'm not saying we should keep them," Amy sighed. "But I do think Daybreak needs a little more time." She glanced up at Ty and their eyes met, just for an instant. Amy looked away again, feeling awkward.

"Well, we don't have to decide today," said Ty, after a pause. "Let's leave them outside while there's still a bit of sun."

"Good idea," Amy agreed, as they turned to walk back between the turn-out paddocks towards the stableyard. On their left, two other horses were nosing the snow for grass to graze.

Ty stopped at the gate. "I think I'll bring Moochie and Jake in now," he said. "They've probably been out long enough."

"OK," said Amy, "I guess that leaves me with the tack-room to sort out."

Ty grinned. Sorting out the tack-room had become everyone's least favourite job. However well they organized it, there just wasn't enough space. "Have fun," he said. "I might come and join you later, if you're lucky."

"Yeah, right," said Amy, laughing. She carried on up the path and headed into the yard.

As she walked into the tack-room, she gazed at the racks, frowning. Most of them had two or three saddles on them, placed carefully on top of each other, but this really wasn't ideal. Another wall was half taken up with the bridles, and half with photos and rosettes. Then there was the table where they cleaned the tack, storage trunks at the back, halters, martingales, lunging equipment... It was all laid out neatly enough, but there was barely room to move.

Just as she was picking up a fallen bridle, Ben came in and dumped a grooming kit into one of the trunks.

"How's it going?" he asked.

"It's not, at the moment," Amy answered. "I'm trying to find us some more space. So how did Red's schooling go today?"

Red was Ben's own horse, a six-year-old chestnut gelding who was turning out to be a really talented showjumper.

"Fine. He's jumping really well." Ben gestured to the left wall of the tack-room. "Why don't you take down those pictures and ribbons and put up more saddle racks?"

"We could, I guess," Amy said slowly. She looked at the pictures — there was one of her on Sundance, her mother, Marion, on Pegasus, and a whole row of other horses who'd come and gone under her mother's care. Amy didn't even remember some of them — she'd been too young. And now that both her mom and Pegasus were gone, perhaps it would be best to take the pictures down, as Ben suggested.

"Or maybe just some of them," Ben added, looking at Amy's thoughtful face.

Amy smiled quickly. "No, it's a good idea," she agreed. "I'll see how Lou and Grandpa feel about it. And check out what we can afford for racking."

Amy headed into the farmhouse and kicked off her boots. Quickly, she went through to the office where her older sister, Lou, was staring intently at the laptop in front of her.

"Hi there," Amy said, peering in through the doorway. "I've just been having a think about the tack-room. Ben suggested we take down the pictures and put up some new racks. It would help – for now, at least."

"Sorry?" Lou answered absent-mindedly. She started to type rapidly, her blue eyes never wavering from the screen.

"New saddle racks," Amy repeated. "The tack-room's so full we're having to pile saddles on top of each other."

"Oh – right," Lou said after a pause. "Sounds like a good plan. We could probably find room for the pictures in the house anyway. How much would the racks cost?"

"I'm not sure," Amy said. "Could you find out?" She stepped into the room and peered briefly over Lou's shoulder at the laptop. "Glad you're enjoying your new toy," she teased.

"Toy!" Lou exclaimed. Unlike Amy, she'd grown up in England, and her accent always sounded stronger when she was indignant about something. She looked up, but then she saw Amy's amused expression and smiled. "This is going to make a big difference, Amy Fleming. All the tedious jobs will take a tenth of the time with these new systems. And we can do lots of new things, too."

She pushed the screen around so that Amy could see.

"This is a database of different bedding suppliers. I've thought out a kind of publicity proposal. I was going to get the wording right before showing you, but you might as well see it now."

"Publicity proposal?" Amy asked suspiciously. "What for?"

"For the suppliers. I've been reading about some really good bedding materials that would save you a lot of time on mucking out. The suppliers would use us in their advertising material, and we'd get cheaper bedding," Lou explained. "And we'd get good publicity, too."

"But straw's fine," Amy pointed out. "It's what we've always used."

"Yes. But the advertising would be very useful," said Lou.

"Well – I guess so." Amy hesitated, trying to share Lou's enthusiasm. As far as she was concerned, making sure the horses were cared for was more important than any new computer equipment or advertising deal. Still, she needed to give her sister a chance. "Maybe it's worth giving it a go," she added.

The phone rang, and Lou reached over to answer it. "Of course it is," she smiled. "You'll see."

Amy smiled back, wanting to believe her. She and Lou hadn't always seen eye to eye over the past five months, since Lou had left her job in New York. But things had started to get better, gradually. Now, Lou belonged at Heartland as much as anyone else. Just as she headed for the door again, Amy caught a snatch of Lou's conversation on the phone.

"Well, I appreciate you getting back to me so quickly," Lou was saying. "And Sunday's absolutely fine. No problem."

There was a pause, then Lou added, "Two-thirty suits us too. Yes, thank you. Goodbye."

She put the phone down and turned to Amy with a smile, her cheeks slightly flushed.

"What's going on?" Amy demanded.

"Sit down," said Lou. "This is important."

"Well – OK," Amy said hesitantly. "What is it?"

"A new client. I've found a horse that needs treating."

"A new horse?" Amy looked puzzled. "What do you mean – *you've* found one?"

"Just that," Lou grinned. "I've thought for a long time that maybe we should approach people straight off, rather than wait for them to find us. And now I've managed to do it."

Amy was intrigued. "Go on!" she said. "So who was it on the phone?"

"Do you remember that big fire back in November? The one at that training farm near Baltimore?"

Amy nodded. "Brookland Ridge," she answered. It had been in all the papers.

"That's the one," agreed Lou. "I called them yesterday and explained who we were, and I asked whether they had any horses in need of treatment."

"But aren't they all racehorses?" Amy gasped.

"So?" said Lou. "That shouldn't be a problem, should it?"

"Well…" Amy paused. "I don't know – it's just that racehorses can be really highly strung."

Lou's face fell slightly.

Amy took a deep breath. "You should have discussed this with me first, Lou," she said, trying not to sound annoyed.

"I'm sorry. You're right. To be honest I didn't think they'd say yes so quickly." Lou's eyes met her sister's.

"Well, tell me about the horse," Amy sighed.

Lou paused. "He's called Gallant Prince."

"Gallant Prince!" Amy exclaimed. The horse had been one of the top three-year-olds last season. He'd won the Maryland Breeders' Cup at Pimlico. Then he'd been caught in the fire and become a hero by breaking free and alerting his stable lad, saving many other horses. But he'd paid a tragic price in the form of his own injuries – his tendons had been so badly damaged by the fire that he'd never race again.

"So what's happened since the fire?" Amy asked. "Did they tell you?"

Lou nodded slowly. "He went to a specialist equine centre to be treated for the burns, but there's nothing more they can do for him. He's quite deeply scarred, and he'll always be unsound. It's the emotional side that's the real problem – no one can get anywhere near him. I spoke to the trainer, Luke Norton, who sounded at his wits' end," Lou explained. "The fire's completely traumatized the horse, and nothing they do seems to work. If only we can help him, he might be able to go to stud. The owner has a farm – he's so attached to the horse that he doesn't want to lose him."

Amy thought for a moment. Gallant Prince would be an amazing horse to work with – and if she could cure him... She took a deep breath.

"We'd have to keep him separate from the mares," she said.

"Could we manage that?" asked Lou, slightly anxiously.

"Let me talk it over with Ty," Amy replied.

Lou looked relieved. "Well, let me know what you decide soon," she said. "If there's a problem, I'll need to know pretty fast. I've said they can bring him here on Sunday."

Chapter Two

"Ty!" Amy called, hurrying out on to the yard. "Ty?"

There was no sign of him, so she headed round to the back barn.

"There you are!" said Amy, looking into Jake's stall, where Ty was unbuckling the bay horse's New Zealand rug. Moochie was already pulling contentedly at his hay net in the stall next to him.

"What is it?" Ty asked, looking surprised at the urgency in her voice.

"D'you remember Gallant Prince? The horse up at Brookland Ridge who was caught in a fire?" Amy said breathlessly.

"Of course I do," said Ty, sliding the rug off Jake's back. "Why?"

"Well, there's a chance he could come to Heartland!"

"Here?" Ty looked puzzled.

"Yeah, what do you think? Lou's spoken to his trainer, Luke Norton. His owner wants to be able to send him to stud, but he's still completely traumatized. No one can get near him."

Ty raised an eyebrow. "I'm not surprised," he commented. "That was a pretty major thing for him to go through." He hesitated. "But we're not really set up to deal with racehorses here, are we?"

Amy understood his reaction. A highly strung thoroughbred was very different from the horses they usually took on, and they were already really busy. "But we've never turned away a damaged horse before," she pointed out.

"True," Ty agreed. He let himself out of Jake's stall with the rug slung over his arm. "And I guess there's no real reason why we should turn away this one. It might be difficult, but..." He trailed off.

Amy felt relieved. "So you agree we should take him?"

"I guess," Ty said slowly. "Though we'll need to decide where to put him."

Amy looked down the wide aisle of the barn. There were six stalls on either side, and another six on the main stableyard.

"He could go at the end," Amy suggested. "We could put the geldings around him." She thought quickly. There was Sundance, Moochie, Pirate, Jake, Crispin, Blackjack ... and Ben's horse, Red. "That would leave us with one free stall. We could have that next to him – to create a gap between him and the other horses. He'd basically be on his own. What do you think?"

"It might work," said Ty, with a shrug. "It's the best we can do with all the other stalls being full."

"OK," said Amy. "But I'd better check that Ben doesn't mind moving Red."

"I'll do that," Ty offered. "And I'll fetch Melody and Daybreak in if you like. It's getting cold."

They headed out of the barn. The sun had just dropped behind the white, weatherboarded farmhouse and the light was fading. Ty headed down the track to the turn-out paddocks, while Amy walked back towards the house, where she could see her grandpa, Jack Bartlett, through the kitchen window. He was obviously talking to Lou.

"Grandpa! Has Lou told you about Gallant Prince?" she asked as she came in through the door.

"She has," Jack said, smiling. "Kind of a new direction for us, isn't it?" He looked shrewdly at Amy, his eyes narrowing thoughtfully. "It's a lot to take on. You'll need to make sure he doesn't take over too much. Especially as we'll probably get a fair amount of attention."

"Attention?" Amy echoed.

"Press attention. After all, he's been in the papers plenty," said Grandpa.

Amy realized that he was right. The Gallant Prince story was well known locally, and people would be curious about what was happening to him next.

"But that won't make any difference to how we treat him," Amy said.

"No," Grandpa agreed. "Well, it shouldn't. He's a horse that needs help, like any other. But it might be difficult to remember that. You'll be under a lot of pressure, Amy."

Amy felt a pang of anxiety at his words. It was impossible to know exactly how difficult Prince was going to be without meeting him first. But they'd coped with badly traumatized horses before. She was sure it would be all right. Gallant Prince needed them. It *had* to be all right.

"Are you OK with that?" Lou asked Amy, concerned. "If it's too much, I can always ring Mr Norton."

"No," Amy said determinedly. "I'm sure we can cope. It sounds like we're his last hope. We'll take him."

"Where were you this morning?" Amy demanded in a low voice as Soraya slid into the desk beside her. It was Monday morning, and Soraya hadn't been on the school bus as usual. "Have I got some news to tell you!"

"Dentist," Soraya lisped back, giving a weird lopsided smile. Amy realized she couldn't speak properly because one side of her face was numb. Soraya opened her school bag and pulled out her history books. "Why? What's happened?"

With one eye on the teacher, Amy grinned excitedly. "We've got a racehorse coming to Heartland," she said.

"A racehorse!" Soraya stared at her friend, her brown eyes wide with amazement.

Amy nodded, as their history teacher caught her eye. She turned back to her books. "I'll tell you afterwards."

Soraya gave her an impatient look, but turned to concentrate on what the teacher was writing on the board.

It wasn't until the lesson came to a close that Soraya had a chance to hear the whole story. They shoved their books in their bags and headed for the door.

"So tell me," said Soraya, as soon as they were in the corridor.

"It's Gallant Prince," Amy answered.

"As in — *the* Gallant Prince?" Soraya asked. "The one that was in the fire?"

"That's the one," said Amy. "Apparently he's been totally unmanageable since the fire. So we're taking him on."

Soraya looked impressed. "Amy, that's amazing," she began.

"What's amazing?" said a voice behind them. They looked round to see their friend Matt Trewin — with Ashley Grant at his side. Things had been a bit strained with Matt since Ashley's Christmas party, when he'd asked Amy to start dating him. Amy had felt awkward. She'd always thought of him as one of her best friends, but nothing more. Now, he was dating Ashley — whom Amy couldn't stand.

"Hi there, Matt," said Soraya.

"Well, come on, what's the news?" demanded Matt.

Amy longed to tell him all about Gallant Prince, but she didn't want to talk to him about Heartland with Ashley standing there. Ashley's mother ran a stables called Green

Briar, which used very different methods from Heartland, and Ashley never missed a chance to put Amy down.

"Oh, nothing much," Amy said lightly. "So who's done their biology homework?" she went on, changing the subject.

"Why? Want some help from Matt? Now there's a surprise," Ashley chipped in.

Amy stared at her. Matt and Soraya were usually good-humoured about helping her out when she was short of time, and it was none of Ashley's business. "I've finished it, actually," Amy retorted.

"Now that *is* news!" Matt grinned, teasingly.

He and Ashley sauntered off, and Amy watched them go in astonishment. She still didn't understand why Matt liked Ashley so much. She was awful! But he just didn't seem to see it.

"*Have* you finished your homework?" Soraya asked, when they were out of earshot.

"Of course not," said Amy. "Can you give me a hand?"

"Sure thing." Soraya smiled. "We'll do it at lunch."

But even with Soraya helping her, Amy had trouble concentrating that day. Her mind kept drifting back to the stallion. What would he be like? How badly damaged would he be? She tried to imagine the terror of a horse caught in a fire, and shuddered. It would take a long time for any horse to recover from that. Amy pictured the beautiful horse she'd watched last season on TV. Gallant Prince must look pretty different now. What would he be like? Would he respond to her? Where was she going to begin?

As Amy hurried up Heartland's long driveway that afternoon, she felt a sense of relief that the school day was over. A car passed her on the way, heading in the opposite direction. Amy watched it go, then went into the farmhouse.

"Lou!" she called as soon as she entered the kitchen. "Lou? Who was that?"

"I'm through here," came Lou's voice from the sitting room.

Amy went through and was surprised to see the armchairs arranged opposite each other in a formal line. Lou was putting photo albums back on the bookshelf.

"What's been going on?" Amy asked.

"We've had a reporter here," Lou answered, looking excited. "We're going to be in the *Richmond Post*."

"The *Richmond Post*?" Amy looked astonished.

"Uh-huh," said Lou. "And all because of Gallant Prince."

"But how did they find out so fast?" Amy gasped.

Lou shrugged, picking up empty coffee cups from the table. "I guess word must have got out from Brookland Ridge."

"So what did the reporter ask? Prince isn't even here yet."

"All sorts of stuff about Heartland. How we work. About Mom, and what happened…"

"Well, I guess that's OK," said Amy, taking a deep breath.

"It can't do us any harm," Lou agreed, grinning.

Amy tried to put Prince to the back of her mind when she started the yard chores the next morning. She headed for Melody and Daybreak's stall first.

"Hi, girl," she said softly to Melody as she slipped a halter over Daybreak's ears. "I'm going to take your baby for a walk."

As she led the little filly out of the stall, Melody whickered anxiously. Daybreak was already looking around eagerly, excited to be out. Amy led her up the yard, then asked her to stop. The foal halted obediently, and Amy began her routine of running her hands over Daybreak's body and asking her to pick her feet up, one at a time. When Daybreak was older, she'd have to have her hooves picked out regularly and her feet shod, so it was important that she knew what to expect, and got used to balancing on three legs. Daybreak was eager to please, and nuzzled Amy affectionately.

"Good girl," said Amy, picking up one of her forelegs.

"She looks relaxed!" Ben commented, as he came out of the feed-room.

"Yes," Amy agreed, "we're getting there. Are you busy?"

"Well, I was going to lunge Red, but it can wait a while," he said. "Why?"

"I was wondering if you might handle Daybreak," said Amy. "She still needs to work a little more with other people."

"Sure," Ben nodded.

"Great," said Amy. "Ten or fifteen minutes will be plenty.

It might be good if I'm not around, but if you need me, I'll be in the tack-room."

"OK," Ben said, taking the lead-rope. "I'll come and find you if I need to."

Amy headed into the crowded tack-room. She realized that she hadn't had time to ask Grandpa how he felt about moving the pictures, and made a mental note to have a word with him later. She was just working up a shine on Sundance's saddle when Ty peered in. Amy met his gaze, and smiled. They'd hardly seen each other all week — there had been so much to do. But now they were alone.

"How's it going?" he asked softly.

"Not bad," said Amy. "I've just been working Daybreak, and now Ben's with her. You're moving the geldings today, aren't you?"

She reached out for the saddle soap, but it slipped and fell to the floor near Ty's feet. He picked it up and stepped closer to hand it back. Amy took it from him, blushing slightly. She knew that Ty had been trying to find the right moment to talk to her ever since Christmas Eve, when they'd kissed. But she didn't know what to say. Ty was really special to her, but she wasn't sure what it all meant. And the last thing she wanted was to be like the other girls at school, mooning over a boyfriend all the time.

"Amy —" Ty began.

"Ty, I —" she started, at the same time. They both stopped, and looked at each other.

"Amy, I think Daybreak's had enough," Ben's voice came from the doorway, making them both jump. "Shall I put her in her stall?"

"No, I can do that," Amy said, feeling relieved at the interruption. "Was she OK with you?" She brushed gently past Ty and stepped back into the yard.

"Yeah, she was fine," said Ben. "Melody's looking a bit stressed, though."

Amy turned to see Melody peering over her half-door, craning her neck anxiously to keep an eye on her daughter. "She'll be OK now," said Amy. She knew she should go back into the tack-room and talk things through with Ty, but something stopped her … something was holding her back. What if things went wrong between them? Somehow it seemed a whole lot easier to carry on just the way they were – the way they'd always been. Taking hold of Daybreak's halter, she led her back up the yard and into her stall.

By the time Amy came out, Ty was already leading Pirate out of the yard towards the back barn. Amy felt unsettled. She regretted not talking to him, and a little voice inside her whispered, *Something has changed. Things aren't the same any more.* She tried to push the thought to the back of her mind and quickly headed back to the tack room. There really was too much to get on with. She'd have to think about Ty later…

* * *

By late morning, Amy was starving. As she went in search of food in the kitchen, she realized that Lou was on the phone. It sounded like she was talking to Scott Trewin, her boy-friend. He was Matt's brother, and the local equine vet. Amy headed for the fridge and started putting things on the table for lunch, trying not to listen to the conversation.

"It's *not* that, Scott," Lou was saying in a heated voice. "It's nothing personal. You must be able to see that."

It wasn't like Lou and Scott to argue, and Amy felt embarrassed. "At least it *is* a system," she heard Lou say next. "And if it's going to work, we have to apply it to everyone. Why does it bug you so much?"

As she put some ham and a slab of cheese on the table, Amy spotted the *Richmond Post* on the worktop. She reached for it eagerly and started leafing through it to find the article on Heartland. Lou hung up the phone and sat down. "It's on page four," she told Amy, still sounding annoyed from the phone call. She paused. "I just don't know why Scott's making such a fuss."

Amy looked up. "What d'you mean — making a fuss? What about?"

"Oh, I sent out letters to all our creditors, saying that in future Heartland would pay all bills at the end of the month," Lou said. "You know — just a standard formal letter. Scott says he'd rather keep to the old system, so I said there wasn't really what I'd call a system before. And now there is, and he's part of it."

"Well," Amy began cautiously, "Scott has been Heartland's vet for years."

"Yes," said Lou, sounding exasperated. "But this is much more efficient."

Amy looked doubtfully at her sister. She wasn't sure what to say. She turned to the paper again and spotted the article.

FINAL BETS ON GALLANT PRINCE

Since the fire that destroyed half of Brookland Ridge, the hero of the night, Gallant Prince, has been impossible to handle. His only hope lies in a training farm called Heartland. Here, it's claimed, even the wildest horses are pacified.

Amy frowned. Heartland was much more than a training farm — and she didn't much like the word "pacified", either. Gaining a horse's trust was about building a relationship, not just forcing a horse to calm down. She read on.

Heartland was established as a centre for damaged horses twelve years ago by Marion Fleming, who died tragically last year. Despite her death, work at Heartland has continued. With this prestigious new arrival, all eyes will be on the stables. Its reputation may rise or fall, depending on how it manages the traumatized stallion, one of Baltimore's local heroes.

Amy looked up, appalled. "This is terrible!" she exclaimed. "Its reputation may rise or fall?"

"I know," Lou sighed. "They just picked out what they wanted to hear."

A knot of anxiety clutched at Amy's stomach. "Grandpa's right. They sure know how to put the pressure on, don't they?"

Chapter Three

"If any journalists turn up before Gallant Prince arrives, don't let them in," Grandpa warned. "He's going to be upset enough from the journey as it is."

"There's no question of it," Lou reassured him. "If any more show up, we'll send them away. It'll be easier once he's here — we can shut the gates."

"Interest will probably die down once he's settled in," Amy added. "They won't want to be hanging around the stables just waiting for something to happen."

"No," Grandpa agreed. He looked around the table, where everyone was sitting for Sunday lunch. "We all need to be clear, though, that we're keeping publicity to a minimum from now on. One newspaper article's enough."

"Sure," said Ty. "That makes sense." Beside him, Ben nodded.

Amy let out a sigh of relief that Grandpa was being so firm about this. But she was still nervous, and didn't really feel much like eating. She pushed her roast chicken to one side and put her knife and fork down.

"Right, well, I'll get on," said Ty, clearing his throat. "I'll make sure I'm around for two-thirty."

He stood up and put his boots on, and Lou started clearing away the table. Ben and Amy got up to help her.

"Leave this to me," said Lou. "You head out. You've got enough to do on the yard."

The horsebox arrived promptly. As Amy heard it making its way up the driveway, Lou appeared from the farmhouse. It stopped just inside the stableyard. Two men got out, one in his fifties, the other about Ty's age.

"Louise Fleming?" asked the older man.

Lou stepped forward. "That's me," she said.

"Luke Norton," said the man, shaking her hand. "We spoke on the phone."

Lou nodded and smiled, then immediately turned to indicate Amy and Ty. "This is my sister, Amy Fleming, and Ty Baldwin. They'll be looking after Gallant Prince."

Luke Norton turned to them, looking them up and down. "So who'll be treating him?" he asked.

"That's what I meant," Lou said quickly.

Luke Norton raised an eyebrow and ran a hand impatiently through his thinning hair, then shrugged. "Well, as long as

you're up to it. Where's Prince going to be stabled?" he
went on.

"In the back barn," said Ty.

"OK." Luke Norton nodded, then turned to the stable
lad. "Let's get him out, Sam." The lad nodded and started to
undo the bolts on the horsebox.

Amy watched Sam anxiously, half-listening to Luke Norton,
who had folded his arms and launched into a description of the
accident.

In her mind's eye, Amy saw the fire. She saw the horses
whinnying, their eyes rolling, the smoke sending them
frantic with panic ... and Prince rearing up through the
flames to break down his door, his hooves splintering the
wood, his terror growing as the heat intensified...

The noise of the ramp being lowered brought Amy
back to attention. She stepped forward and looked into
the dark interior, feeling puzzled. She had expected to hear
the stamping of hooves at least, but all was quiet within
the box. Sam appeared at the top of the ramp, leading the
stallion. Amy was astonished. Prince didn't seem remotely
unmanageable. If anything, he seemed placid and gentle as
he gingerly descended, limping with each step.

Amy swallowed. The beautiful racehorse she remembered
from Pimlico was barely recognizable. There was a big scar
down the right side of his face, and the burned areas on his
forelegs and shoulder were clear to see. She turned quickly
to Luke Norton.

"He seems very quiet," she commented. "Is he tran-quillized?"

Luke nodded. "It's the only way we could get him to travel."

Amy exchanged a quick glance with Ty. Of course – it made sense. If Prince was as traumatized as they had said, it would be dangerous to take him anywhere in a horsebox without something to keep him calm. As Sam brought him to a halt in front of them, she studied his lowered head and dull, spiritless eyes, then she stepped forward to gently touch his face with its zigzag white scar.

"Prince," she whispered. He stared at her dully, and stepped back.

"There's a boy," said Sam. "Steady."

Prince stood still again, his head drooping.

Amy looked at Sam. "Are you his stable lad?" she asked.

Sam shook his head and looked awkward. "No, that was Ryan Bailey's job. He used to look after him."

"Used to?" Amy echoed.

"Ryan's left the farm," Luke Norton answered for him, and then, as if that was an end to the matter, he turned to Sam. "OK, let's get him stabled before he starts playing up."

Ty and Amy showed Sam the way round to the back barn and let Prince into his stall. The stallion shifted his weight off his damaged leg and nosed unenthusiastically at his hay net. The geldings further up the barn sensed the presence of the new arrival and whickered excitedly, but Prince barely flicked an ear in their direction.

"Good boy," Amy said softly. She turned to Sam again. "There's no sign of the tranquillizer wearing off yet," she said. "Do you know what he was given?"

"Yeah. It was an ACP. We gave it to him a couple of hours ago, just before we set off."

"It should wear off in another couple of hours then," Ty observed.

"Most likely," said Sam. "Then you'll have to watch out!"

"What d'you mean?" Amy asked quickly.

"He gets pretty wound up," Sam said, sounding serious. "I don't know what anyone can do for him, to be honest." He shrugged. "I'll get the rest of his stuff. Where d'you want me to put it?"

"I'll show you," said Ty. "The tack-room is on the main yard."

Amy and Ty followed Sam back to the horsebox. Amy joined Lou, who was still talking to Luke Norton. "We just can't predict how long we'll need to keep him here," she was saying politely. "But obviously we'll let you know how we're getting on. Each horse's needs are different – we have to get to know them individually and find out what's best for them."

"OK. Whatever," said Luke. "I'll let Mr Hartley know. He's the owner." He shrugged. "He's the one paying for all this."

"We'll certainly call you," Amy assured him.

"Yeah, well, see how you go with him," Luke said briefly. "He can be a bit difficult."

He turned towards the horsebox to check on Sam, who had finished unloading and was lifting the ramp back up into place.

"Ready when you are, Sam," said Luke. He jumped up into the driver's seat and started the engine. Sam clambered up beside him with a wave, and Luke turned the box round.

"I wonder what they mean by difficult?" Amy mused, as the horsebox disappeared down the winding drive.

Ty shrugged. "I guess we should just wait and see," he said as they headed back to the barn.

They turned the corner to the barn and looked into Gallant Prince's stall. Amy studied the racehorse's slender face. His fine lines suggested a deeply sensitive, receptive personality. It was hard to believe that he was really that unmanageable.

"We can carry on treating his physical wounds to start with. Pain always makes any other problems worse," said Ty.

"Scott's coming this afternoon to check him over as well," Amy told him. "We can ask him what he thinks."

Scott arrived an hour later and whistled in disbelief as he took in the stallion's scars. He entered Prince's stall and gently ran his hand down his damaged forelegs. The stallion shifted, but otherwise didn't react.

"He's still tranquillized," Scott commented. "Can we walk him out?"

"Sure," said Amy. "I'll lead him."

In the yard, Scott studied the stallion's uneven, cautious movement.

"Well, the injuries are pretty much healed," he said. "He'll always be unsound, but that shouldn't stop him exercising. Racehorses are bred to be exercised intensively from an early age – they can get upset and restless if they're kept in. They put on weight quickly, too, but it doesn't look as though Prince has done much of that." He lifted one of Prince's eyelids. The horse showed no resistance. Scott looked up. "How long has he been here?" he asked Amy.

"About an hour," said Amy.

"The tranquillizer will start wearing off in another hour or so," he said, examining the stallion's dull eyes again. "Any idea what he's normally like?"

"We haven't been told anything specific. Just that he's unmanageable," Amy admitted.

Scott looked serious. "It's difficult to tell how much of an effect the drug's had on him, but call me if you need any help when it wears off. I'd best head off now if I'm going to get through my other visits." He hesitated, and then gave a wry smile. "Oh, and by the way, tell Ms Fleming I'll send the invoice through as requested. And tell Lou I'll give her a call later – when I'm through with evening surgery."

* * *

As the afternoon wore on, Amy and Ty checked regularly on Prince in between the other chores. Amy noticed that their new resident was getting more restless. Dark storm clouds were gathering in the sky, so dusk came early – by which time Prince was pacing anxiously around his stall.

"We're going to have to keep a close eye on him," she said to Ty. "A storm's upsetting at the best of times. It might be an idea to give him his feed now. And I'll add some Rescue Remedy to his water – it might calm him down."

"We could try another of the Bach Flower Remedies, too," suggested Ty. "I think walnut remedy should help him settle. Check what the book says, though; I haven't used it for a while."

Amy went to the feed-room and mixed the stallion's feed in a bucket, then she picked a well-used book off the shelf and flicked through to the index. It was her mother's guide to Bach Flower Remedies, which she and Ty referred to constantly.

Walnut helps adjustment to change, either in circumstances or environment.

Perfect, thought Amy. She looked along the shelf of little brown bottles and picked out two, putting them in her pocket. She would add four drops of walnut and six of Rescue Remedy to Prince's drinking water. As she stepped out of the feed-room, heavy drops of rain began to hit the yard. She ran to the barn where she could already hear Prince stumbling around his stall. Just as she was about to draw back the bolt, there was a crack of thunder and the lighting cut out. The stalls were plunged into darkness.

Amy gasped. Suddenly she heard a frantic whinny. Gallant Prince! In the last, fading shreds of daylight, she saw the rolling whites of the stallion's eyes and the flash of his hooves as he reared up. He crashed down with his forelegs against the door of the stall, and reared again, letting out another high-pitched whinny. As his forelegs smashed into the door again, Amy heard the sound of splintering wood...

Chapter 4

"Ty! *Ty!*" Amy dropped the feed bucket and raced out of the barn. "There's been a blackout!"

Just at that moment, the power came back on. Light flooded the yard. Amy stopped in her tracks and rushed back inside, the desperate sounds of the stallion still echoing around the barn. As she approached Gallant Prince's stall, Amy could see that the horse's coat was completely covered in sweat. His face was tight with panic, his nostrils flaring red. He plunged around his stall, then reared again.

Amy caught sight of a stream of blood running down his foreleg. "Prince! Easy, boy!" she called, but the stallion took no notice.

"He's completely lost it," Amy cried breathlessly as Ty appeared at her side. "And now it's upsetting the geldings —"

Amy turned and saw Ben rushing through the barn door. "Ben!" she shouted.

"What's going on?" he called, running down the aisle.

"Can you see to the other horses? Try to calm them — we'll deal with Prince."

"Sure," said Ben, quickly grasping the situation.

Amy turned again to look at the stallion.

"We have to stand as close as possible," said Ty. "He has to know that we're not going to leave him, however long he carries on like this. He has to be able to trust us."

Amy nodded. There was little else they could do. As Prince continued his blind course around the stall, they called continuously, keeping their voices calm and soothing.

After another fifteen minutes, he began to show signs of exhaustion, and his movements slowed. Eventually, he stood still, trembling, at the back of his stall, the whites of his eyes still rolling, his sides heaving.

"I'll try going in," said Amy.

Cautiously, she pulled back the bolt, and immediately the stallion plunged forward. Amy hastily rebolted the door. She and Ty stood, waiting until Prince slowed and stopped once more. Amy watched him intently for any signs of change, but the only difference was his exhaustion.

"We'd better get hold of Scott fast," said Ty. "He'll need to take a look at that leg."

"You ring him," said Amy. "I'll stay here."

"OK," said Ty. "I've left my mobile in the kitchen. I'll be as quick as I can."

As Ty disappeared off, Amy leaned over the half-door,

studying the stallion. Even though he had come to a halt, he still looked completely stressed out. What if he was always like this when he wasn't tranquillized? Amy felt her stomach knot with anxiety as she faced the prospect of being unable to do anything.

Ty re-entered the barn. "Scott's stuck at Garston Farm delivering a calf – he says he'll be another two hours at least."

"We'll just have to stay here then," said Amy.

"Absolutely," Ty agreed. "Lou says she'll bring some supper out to the barn."

Amy let her breath out, slowly. She realized she was trembling – the horse's distress had been so overwhelming. "Thanks," she said, slightly shakily. "If you hadn't been here –"

"Hey…" Ty stepped forward, and touched her arm. "I'm always here, Amy. You know that."

Amy nodded gratefully, and turned away. She didn't want to think about his words too much. Not right now. She looked back at Gallant Prince. Despite his exhaustion, the horse had started to pace restlessly around his stall once more…

"I'm going to have to give him a shot of domo and torb," said Scott. "That's a sedative which should calm him down straight away. It'll be impossible to get near his leg otherwise."

"OK," said Amy. She didn't like the idea of tranquillizing Prince, but she could see that Scott was right – there was no alternative. "Ty and I should be able to hold on to him."

"Can I help?" Lou offered.

"We can manage," said Amy. She and Ty held fast to Prince's halter while Scott quickly inserted the needle. As if by magic, Prince's breathing slowed and his head dropped. Scott quickly cleaned and disinfected the reopened wound on his leg and bandaged it.

"I'll stay with him," Amy said, when he'd eventually finished. "I'll get some blankets and sleep in the empty stall next door."

"I don't think you need to do that," Ty said gently.

"No, you look exhausted, Amy," Lou agreed.

"I can't leave him," Amy insisted. "Not when he's been this upset. And I think someone should be nearby when the drug wears off, in case he goes crazy again."

"Well, if you're sure…" Ty looked doubtful.

"Of course I'm sure. It's not the first time I've slept out here. You go home. We need someone to be awake and alert in the morning."

"Well … OK," Ty agreed reluctantly.

"Make sure you've got your mobile, Amy," said Lou, looking worried. "Then at least you can call any of us if you need to."

"Yes. Call me any time," said Scott. "I'd better be off now as well."

Amy slept badly. Prince didn't freak out again, but she was woken in the early hours by the sound of him pacing around his stall. As soon as it began to get light, she got up to check on him. The horse looked terrible – his head hanging low, his feed untouched. It was clear that he no longer had any energy.

"Hi there, boy," she said softly, holding out her hand for him to sniff. He shifted his weight away from her. She moved closer. Immediately, Gallant Prince started. He threw his head up and shot to the back of his stall.

Amy stood patiently, then tried moving a step closer once more. This time, the thoroughbred flattened his ears and lunged at her with his teeth. Amy backed off hurriedly. Feeling frustrated, she let herself out of the stall. She stared at him as he eyed her, snorting nervously. After a few minutes, Amy lay back down next door, feeling helpless, her head heavy with tiredness.

At seven o'clock, Lou appeared at the stall with a mug of hot chocolate. "Did you get any sleep?" she asked, sounding concerned.

"Some. Not much," Amy admitted, taking a swig of the hot drink. "It got pretty cold, and Prince kept waking me up." She heard the door of Ty's pick-up slam as he arrived for work.

He came straight round to the barn. "How are you doing?" he asked.

"I'm OK," said Amy, grinning weakly. "But Prince is still really stressed. He hardly rested at all during the night. And he still won't let me get near him."

Ty looked at Amy sympathetically. "You look like you've had a rough night too," he commented.

Amy shrugged. "It was definitely the blackout that spooked him, but I'm wondering if he's worse when it's dark generally," she said. "After all, the fire happened at night. Maybe we could try improving the lighting in the stall – like, try a different kind of bulb? An orange glow would be really calming."

Ty looked thoughtful. "Well – OK. It's a start. I'll set it up while you're at school."

"Great," said Amy. "And I'll make up a bran mash for him and put some mint in it. That might tempt him to eat, if he calms down for long enough."

Amy tried not to think about how tired she was as she went about the usual chores of feeding all of the horses and mucking out.

"Amy, I'll finish off the front yard stalls," Ben offered. "You look all in. And you need to get ready for school."

"Thanks, Ben, but I'm fine," Amy insisted, although she felt weary. The last thing she wanted was to do was spend the day stuck behind a desk, but she didn't have much choice.

"You're running late," Ben pointed out gently.

Amy looked at her watch in alarm. He was right. The time had flown by. She dashed into the farmhouse to get ready, making it to the bus stop with only seconds to spare.

"Amy," said Soraya, looking concerned. "You don't look

so good." She and Amy were sitting at one of the cafeteria tables during lunch. Amy kept drifting away as tiredness overcame her.

"Well, neither would you, if you'd been up half the night with a crazy horse," Amy answered, realizing that she hadn't even brushed her hair that morning. She rarely looked totally tidy, but today she must look a state. "Do you have a hairbrush with you?"

"Sure," said Soraya. She rummaged in her bag and fished one out. "So Prince is in a bad way, huh?" she asked.

"Yeah," Amy admitted. "He completely lost it. It was awful seeing him so worked up. I don't know how I'd have coped if Ty hadn't been there."

"I'm not surprised," said Soraya, with feeling. "I'd have been scared too. I'm really impressed that you stayed out all night with him."

"I couldn't leave him," Amy said simply. She sighed, then frowned as she saw Ashley Grant making her way over to them. For once, she wasn't with Matt. Amy wondered briefly if Matt might be having a good influence on her, but the stuck-up expression on Ashley's face immediately gave her the answer to that.

"Why, hello, Amy," said Ashley, flicking her hair over her shoulder. "How are things at Heartland?"

"Fine, thank you," Amy responded coolly, wondering what Ashley wanted. There was sure to be *something*.

"Really? I understand you've been creating a few problems

for yourself. It's not surprising, I suppose."

"What are you're talking about?" Amy demanded.

Ashley smirked. "A racehorse is totally different from one of your nice little riding ponies, you know," she said in a superior tone. "What makes you think you can cope? I mean, you barely even go to the races. When did I last see *you* at Belmont Park?"

Amy glared at Ashley. It was hardly worth responding. "I like to get my priorities right, Ashley," she said coldly.

"Well, you're looking a bit rough at the edges, Amy. Maybe you should get yourself some sleeping pills. You and Gallant Prince could share them," Ashley purred. Then she turned on her heel and sauntered off.

"That beats *everything*," Amy muttered.

"But how does she know you're having trouble?" asked Soraya, outraged. "Prince only arrived yesterday."

"Well, we were in the papers on Saturday." Amy hesitated. But Soraya was right. It was as though Ashley had known exactly what had happened last night. They looked at each other. The thought dawned on both of them at the same time.

"Matt," they said together.

Amy felt stung. She couldn't help it. It was hardly surprising that Matt knew — after all, he was Scott's brother, but even so...

"How *could* he!" she exclaimed.

"He probably didn't think there was anything secret about

it," said Soraya, trying to be helpful. "The whole thing's big news. And I bet Ashley interrogated him, anyway."

"But he must have known she'd leap on it like a vulture," Amy protested.

"He likes her," said Soraya. "And I guess that means he trusts her."

Amy groaned. It seemed incredible. As far as she was concerned, Ashley Grant was bad news.

"Amy! Come and check this out!" Ty called over, as Amy headed up the aisle of the back barn that evening. Ty and Jack Bartlett were bent over something on the ground.

Amy hurried over. "What are you doing?" she asked curiously. Grandpa was fiddling with some crocodile clips on an old car battery.

"It's all set," Jack said, straightening up and smiling. "Well, I'm heading in. I don't want to miss Monday-night football on TV — Ty can explain it all to you, Amy."

"OK, thanks, Grandpa," said Amy, as Jack headed off out of the barn. "So what's going on?" she asked, turning to Ty and gesturing at the battery.

"It's in case we get another power cut," Ty explained. "Jack's set up a relay switch, just for Prince's stall. The car battery will power the bulb until the main power comes back on."

"Good idea," said Amy.

"And we've put in that orange bulb," Ty went on. "It

should make a difference to the feel of his stall, as well."

"How has he been today?" Amy asked. She looked over the half-door at Prince, who stayed at the back of his stall. "Did he eat much of the mash I made him this morning?"

"Some," said Ty. "But he left most of it. He's been incredibly jumpy, but at least he hasn't done anything crazy."

Amy looked at the stallion's staring coat. She could see his ribs. He obviously wasn't eating enough, but until he calmed down, he wasn't likely to, either. She sighed. "We need to work out what it is that really spooks him," she said.

"I'd be surprised if it's something in particular," said Ty. "He's in such a state, anything sudden or different would trigger him."

"Do you think so?" mused Amy. "I'd understand him getting worse when it's dark – I mean, the fire was at night. If that's true, we could try rock rose remedy – that's supposed to soothe night-time fears."

"I guess so," said Ty slowly. "But he's not exactly chilled out in daylight, either."

Amy turned to the half-door again and leaned over it, studying the stallion. Prince started at her movement, then began pacing around, eyeing Amy and Ty nervously.

"Even us standing here talking seems to upset him," said Amy. "He's just so tense. The walnut remedy should help with that, though – and we could add some crab apple to help him come to terms with his injuries. But they're not going to be enough on their own. We need to make some sort of contact with him. We ought to try T-touch – Daybreak loved massage treatment."

Ty nodded. "I've been thinking that myself – only whenever I try to get near him, he just breaks into a sweat and shies away from me."

"Well, I guess he's only been here a couple of days. He still needs to settle in," said Amy. "We'll just have to keep trying. I'll come back and try later – right now, I need to do some work with Daybreak before it gets dark."

Amy couldn't be sure, but at the mention of Daybreak, something like irritation seemed to flit across Ty's face.

"Ben led her out earlier," he said.

"Oh, right," said Amy. "Well, I'll just take her out once more – she can handle a couple of sessions a day."

Ty shrugged. "I don't really think it's necessary."

"The more handling she gets, the better," said Amy, feeling slightly defensive. "I'll only be fifteen minutes. Then I'll start mixing the feeds."

Seeing the bright-eyed little filly was a pleasure for Amy after the difficulties over Gallant Prince. She felt her heart warm as Daybreak's muzzle butted her affectionately. Amy led her out into the yard and went through the usual routine. As she ran her hand down the back of each leg, Daybreak knew automatically what to do and lifted her hoof almost without being asked. Amy finished the session with a few moments of T-touch massage, working over the foal's body in light circles with her fingers. Daybreak stood still, loving the attention.

"She's looking great," said Ty, giving Amy a grin as he passed by.

"She's getting there," Amy agreed, smiling back.

Dusk was falling by the time Amy put Daybreak back into her stall. Her mind turned back to the stallion. She went to find Ty, who was already mixing the evening feeds. "I think maybe I should have a go at T-touch with Prince now, before it gets any darker," she said. "It'll be completely dark if I wait till after the feeds."

"That's true," he agreed. "I'll come and watch, in case you need a hand with him."

They headed into the barn, where Prince was still pacing anxiously around his stall. He threw his head up and snorted as Amy carefully drew back the bolt and let herself in.

"Steady, boy," she murmured softly. He stood still at the back of the stall and stared at her. She could see how tense he was — Ty was right, he was ready to spring into panic for the slightest reason. She stepped closer, murmuring in a soothing voice. Prince backed away from her, shaking his head. Amy positioned herself near his shoulder, so he could see her without feeling threatened, and moved closer again. Prince snorted and rolled his eyes at her, but he was right in the corner of the stall and couldn't go back any further. Slowly, Amy took one more step, and raised her arm to touch his neck.

At that moment, Ben came into the barn, the big door banging shut behind him. The stallion started as though he'd been shot. He whinnied wildly and reared up, then plunged past Amy blindly, knocking her to the back of the stall.

"Amy!" Ty cried, shooting back the bolt of the door. "Get out!"

But now Prince was between Amy and the door. She was trapped behind him, and Ty had to hurriedly ram the bolt shut again to prevent the stallion from escaping. Prince whinnied again, and turned around on his haunches. Amy pressed herself up against the back of the stall, her heart pounding.

"Amy!" called Ty desperately. "Climb over the side!"

Amy quickly sized up the side of the stall. There weren't any toe-holds and the concrete blocks reached up to shoulder height. Then there were wooden slats above that. Even if she could manage it, scrambling up there would only distress Prince more. Panic began to rise inside her.

"I — can't," she managed to squeeze out, as Prince gave another piercing whinny, then snaked his neck menacingly in her direction. Acting instinctively, she threw her hands in the air. As she knew it would, it startled Prince all over again. He leaped back and Amy made her move, diving for the half-door as the stallion reared again. Ty reacted instantly to let her out, then banged the door shut behind her. She leaned against it for a few seconds, gasping for breath, as Prince continued to career dangerously around his stall.

"Amy, are you OK?" asked Ben, his face ashen.

Amy nodded. "I just feel awful for startling him again," she said.

"You did exactly the right thing!" exclaimed Ty. "You had to do something."

"But we've *got* to calm him," said Amy. "Or he'll injure himself again."

"Was there anything that worked last night?" Ben asked in a low voice.

Amy shook her head in despair, as Ty tried calling to Prince in a low, soothing voice. It had no effect. The stallion reared and kicked, giving painful high-pitched whinnies, crashing around the confined space of the stall. Then he stopped, staring at the three faces at his stall door, but without appearing to really see them. His eyes were still glazed with panic. He stood still, his legs splayed, his nostrils flaring.

"So much for the orange bulb," Ty muttered.

"And so much for trying T-touch," said Amy shakily. "But he *was* calmer earlier. The bulb might have made a bit of difference. Maybe there was something about the sound of the door that reminded him of the fire." But deep down, she knew she was clutching at straws. He had panicked for no real reason...

"We're going to have to leave him," said Ty. "You can't stay out here with him every night, Amy. When he loses it, there's nothing you can do – you can't get in there with him. Look what just happened."

Amy nodded miserably. She hated seeing a horse in such

a state of distress. It seemed wrong to leave him on his own, but there was nothing anyone could do when Prince began to panic. Or was there? Deep down, Amy refused to believe that any horse could be completely beyond human reach. There *had* to be a way of communicating with him – but as to finding it, well, that was another matter.

Chapter Five

It was Wednesday evening, and Amy had just got back from school. Every night since Sunday Prince had continued to wreck his stall after nightfall. As he'd settled into his new surroundings, he'd been slightly calmer during daylight, but Ty and Ben were still finding it impossible to groom him or lead him out.

"I think the only answer is join-up," said Amy.

Ty looked dubious. "I'm not sure it's safe to let him loose in the training ring," he warned. "He's so unpredictable."

"But we can't do any close work with him, like T-Touch," Amy pointed out. "And he needs to get some exercise. At least with join-up we don't need to work too close — the whole point is to keep him at a distance until he *chooses* to join-up. You could come and watch out for me — I think it's worth a try."

Join-up was usually the first step in building a solid relationship with a horse. It was a technique that Amy had learned from her mother and, so far, she had never known it to fail.

"I still think it's a bit soon," said Ty. "It's bound to take a few days for the remedies to start working. Maybe we should wait until he's calmer."

Amy thought of being in the training ring on her own with Prince. Despite his injuries, he was still a powerful horse, and Ty was right – even though it wasn't like being trapped in the stall with him, it could be dangerous. But then she thought of Spartan, a horse she had worked with last year. Join-up had worked with him, and he'd been almost as unmanageable as Prince.

"But it might help us make that connection," said Amy.

"I guess you're right," Ty agreed reluctantly. "Do you want to try it now?"

"Why not?" said Amy. "We've still got an hour or so of daylight."

"OK," said Ty, slightly wearily. "You know, Amy, we're going to have treat the geldings, too. The stress is getting to them. Pirate and Red are probably the worst affected. We can turn them out for part of the day, which should help, but they still have to come in at night. I'll talk to Ben about using walnut remedy. That'll help them adjust to change. And maybe some aspen, to keep their anxiety under control."

Amy looked at him seriously, and swallowed. Ty was right.

Prince's frenzied outbursts were affecting the other horses. She knew that Ben didn't want to say anything, but it was easy to tell from his face how anxious he was getting about Red. And Prince's behaviour was the last thing Pirate needed. He had a habit of box-walking, a sure sign of anxiety and stress, and would spend hours pacing round and round his stall. Prince was definitely making him worse.

"Right," she said. "I'll do some T-touch with Pirate once we've worked with Prince." She gave a worried frown. By the time she'd tried join-up, there wouldn't be much time for Pirate. But Prince had to be her priority, she told herself. Didn't he?

Amy headed to her bedroom to change. As she pulled on her jeans, Lou knocked at the door.

"Amy?" she asked. "Can I come in?"

"Sure," Amy said.

Lou stood in the doorway, a worried expression on her face. "Has Grandpa said anything to you about our latest arrival?" she asked.

"No... Why would he?" Amy said, feeling a rush of concern.

Lou sighed. "Well, he came in this afternoon complaining that he'd never seen such a barnful of jittery horses."

Amy took a deep breath and nodded, thinking of her conversation with Ty. She knew Grandpa was right.

"I just thought I'd let you know," said Lou. "I think he's

getting worried, Amy. It's not like Grandpa to make comments like that."

Amy nodded. It was true — Grandpa didn't interfere with the work going on with the horses. He trusted Amy totally. If he was saying things like that to Lou, he *must* be worried. But they just had to keep on going, for the time being. "Thanks for telling me, Lou," said Amy. "It's still early days, though. We're about to try join-up."

On the way down to the main training ring, Prince fought constantly, pulling backwards and tossing his head as Ty gripped the reins tightly under his chin. His face was grim, and Amy could read his thoughts — he didn't think this was a good idea. But they made it, and Amy opened the gate.

"We'll need to knot the reins so he doesn't trip," said Amy. "I'll do that, if you can just hold on to him for a minute longer."

Quickly, Amy fixed the reins so they rested safely halfway up the stallion's neck. Then Ty let Prince go, and walked back to the fence while Amy took up her position in the middle of the ring. She unfurled the long-line in her hand and flicked it gently in Prince's direction.

Prince started violently and reared before heading to the outside of the ring. There, he stopped, staring at Amy, his nostrils flaring. She moved towards him and flicked the line again. Prince set off around the outside of the ring. It was the first time that Amy and Ty had seen Prince moving freely in the open since his arrival. At a trot, the stiffness in his right foreleg was easier to see. His head nodded and his right shoulder dropped slightly – the limp that he would never entirely lose.

Amy squared her shoulders to the stallion's and kept driving him on. By doing this, she was showing him that he would have to keep on working until he chose to trust her. But although Prince was clearly reluctant to keep moving, the subtle signals that indicated the start of join-up weren't happening, either. He wasn't flicking his inside ear towards her, or beginning to relax. He wasn't saying he wanted to stop, and be with her. In fact, he still shied away every time she flicked the long-line in his direction, and rolled his eyes ominously. He seemed determined to stay as far from her as possible, and Amy noticed that his limp was becoming more pronounced the longer she kept him trotting around.

"Ty, I'm going to have to stop," she called, letting her shoulders sag. She looked the stallion in the eye and he snorted, clearly exhausted, but defiant. "We're just not getting anywhere."

Ty jumped down from the fence, where he'd been sitting to watch, and approached Prince cautiously. Amy helped him corner the tired stallion and grab the reins. Amy shook her head. "It's like he just won't respond." Amy shook her head. "It's not that he can't – more that he *won't*. I just can't reach him."

* * *

That night, Amy lay on her bed and stared at the ceiling. Join-up had worked with so many horses over the past months – Promise, Gypsy, Spartan... Prince was the first horse who'd chosen to stay on his own at the outside of the ring.

Spartan – the horse they had been rescuing on the day of her mother's fatal accident. When the tree had crashed on to the pick-up truck and trailer, both Amy and Spartan had been injured. Amy thought back to the afternoon several weeks after the accident when, in a torrential thunderstorm, she had pursued Spartan around and around the ring, giving vent to all her own feelings of anger and loss, until he had given her the signals she had barely expected to see. After that first join-up, he had transformed into a gentle and loving horse again. Amy was the only one who had been able to reach him, because she understood what he had been through.

Amy's thoughts drifted back to Prince. She remembered the pain and defiance in his eyes; she imagined once more the horror of the fire, the desperation to break free ... but she could only *imagine* it. She couldn't *feel* it. Prince was still alone in his terror and his suffering. Perhaps he needed someone who understood like Amy had understood Spartan? Could there be anyone who might? His stable lad? The one who'd left the farm? Maybe he could help? Gradually, Amy began to drift off to sleep. Anything was worth a try.

*   *   *

"Lou!" Amy called up the stairs the next morning, just before she left for the bus stop. "What are you doing on Saturday?"

"I've got a meeting with a rep about new bedding for the stalls," Lou called back. "But that's all."

"Where?" asked Amy. "Near here?"

"No, it's up towards Hagerstown. Why?"

Amy thought quickly. "I just wondered... Would you mind going a bit further, across towards Baltimore? I want to go to Brookland Ridge to talk to that stable lad about Prince – the one that came with him. It's not much further."

Lou appeared at the top of the stairs. She shrugged. "I guess so – it's only another half hour or so. If you really think it'll help..."

"Who knows?" Amy admitted. "But I'm running out of ideas."

Walnut, rock rose and crab apple, Amy muttered to herself in the feed-room on Friday night. *Rescue Remedy*. She looked along the line of brown glass bottles, considering each one, then turned away. At this stage, it was more important to let the remedies they were already using with Prince take effect, rather than keep on trying new ones. They had to be patient.

But being patient was difficult. Earlier that evening, as she was walking Pirate up to the smaller training ring to lunge him, Amy had passed Ben in the main ring, riding Red. As always, they made a striking pair, and she stopped briefly to watch. Ben sat tall in the saddle as he cantered Red in a circle. Red was fighting for his head, snatching at the reins, and Ben looked pale and tense as he encouraged the horse to settle into his stride and accept the bit. Red's neck was lathering up under the reins, until finally Ben slowed him to a trot. He spotted Amy and came over to the fence.

"He's not going so well," Amy commented.

"No," said Ben, frowning. "He's just really wound up. I can't get him to concentrate."

"What's the problem?" Amy asked before she could stop herself.

"He's just being difficult generally," said Ben. He hesitated. "Ever since —" He stopped, and looked away.

Amy felt awkward. *Ever since Prince arrived*, she felt like saying for him. But she couldn't bring herself to voice her thoughts.

"Perhaps you could try some diluted lavender oil with him later," she said quickly. "It might help. Just put some on your fingers and let him sniff it. If he likes it, rub it in gently at the top of his face."

"OK," said Ben, turning Red back towards the centre of the ring. "I'll give it a try. Thanks, Amy."

Amy didn't feel like Ben should be thanking her — especially when the root of Red's problems was so obvious.

* * *

Amy was relieved when Saturday finally arrived and there was something positive she could do. After an early lunch, she and Lou set off towards Baltimore.

"I said I'd be there by three-thirty," said Lou, as she drove down the driveway. "I'll take you up to Brookland Ridge first. We should have plenty of time."

"Who is it you're meeting exactly?" asked Amy, realizing she hadn't taken much notice of Lou's plans.

"It's a company called Champions. They responded to that mail-out I sent round," said Lou. "They produce high-quality bedding, and want to talk to me about the deal I suggested."

"Really?" Amy frowned. "I've never heard of them."

"I think they're new to the area," Lou said.

"So – what kind of bedding do they do?" Amy asked, trying to be positive. She still wasn't sure about Lou's publicity idea.

"It's called SupaDri, and it's meant to be really light and absorbent," said Lou. "I need to check it's as good as they say it is first. I was going to get some samples to bring back and show you. We don't need any *more* bad publicity."

Amy shot her sister a glance. It wasn't like Lou to be pessimistic.

"Well, Prince isn't bringing us bad publicity yet," she said, slightly defensively. But she felt a pang of anxiety all the same. She looked out of the window, her thoughts turning to the stallion. She *had* to find an answer, for everyone's sake.

Lou dropped Amy at the entrance to the training farm. The

words *Brookland Ridge* formed part of an impressive-looking wrought-iron gateway.

"I'll be a couple of hours, I should think," said Lou. "But my mobile's on, anyway, so give me a call if you finish up early." Amy waved and set off up the crisp gravel driveway. She reached the first stable block and looked around. It was quite a sight — the block was charred and blackened, and there was a big gap in the main roof where it had collapsed in the heat of the fire. It felt empty and desolate — no horses looked out over half-doors, and there was none of the usual stable-yard bustle. There was just a lingering smell of burnt wood, and the sound of sawing and hammering from inside one of the stalls.

Amy hurried on to another stable-block that lay through an archway. Here, the stalls all looked as though they were in use, and, at one end, a stable lad was sluicing down the yard with a hose while another swept the water into a drain. Horses pricked their ears and watched her over their stable doors as she walked across the yard to speak to the lads.

"Hi," she greeted them. "I'm looking for Sam."

One of them nodded towards the stalls. "He's grooming," he said.

"Thanks," said Amy, heading for the stall he'd indicated.

Inside, Amy found Sam grooming a big grey mare. He was whistling through his teeth as he worked and didn't hear her approach.

"Hi, Sam," she said, over the half-door. Sam looked up,

startled. "Remember me? I'm Amy Fleming, from Heartland." She hesitated before continuing. "I was wondering if you could help."

Sam gave her a friendly smile, but it soon faded as Amy explained how they were getting on with Prince. "I was wondering if it might be worth talking to his stable lad," Amy finished. "The one who left."

"Ryan?" Sam looked guarded.

"Yes. Do you still see him?" Amy asked.

Sam shook his head. "Nope. None of us do."

"Why not?" Amy probed gently.

Sam looked at her seriously. "You've no idea what happened, have you?" he asked curiously.

"No," Amy admitted. "How could I?"

"Look, Ryan's in a bad way," Sam sighed. "He was pretty badly burned in the fire and he got blamed for what happened."

"Oh, right..." Amy looked thoughtful for a moment. "Just how badly burned?" she asked.

"Pretty bad," Sam replied. "He was blinded in one eye."

Amy was horrified. "Blinded!" she exclaimed, staring at Sam.

Sam nodded. "I know," he said. "We were all pretty shocked."

"But you say he got blamed, as well?"

"Yeah," said Sam awkwardly. "He was the one on duty, the night of the fire. He had to leave, so we all kind of think it's better to steer clear."

Amy didn't know what to say. She watched Sam as he bent down to brush the mare's legs. "But he was close to Prince?" she asked eventually.

"Very close," said Sam. "They were kind of inseparable."

"Listen, Sam," said Amy urgently. "I know you can't get involved, but could you at least tell me how to get in touch with Ryan?"

Sam straightened up. Amy's eyes pleaded with him. "Well... I can't see what harm it'll do," he said. "I'll get his address."

Amy headed back down the driveway. Ryan had been there on the night of the fire – and he had been really close to Prince. Would he able to help the stallion in some way? She pulled her mobile out of her pocket to call Lou.

"I'm not far off," said Lou. "I'll be about twenty minutes."

As she waited on the roadway, Amy studied Ryan's address. Sam had said it wasn't far away.

"Do you think we could go there now?" Amy asked Lou, once she was back in the car. "It'll save another journey later."

Lou looked at her watch. "Sure," she agreed. "As long as we don't take too long."

The house wasn't difficult to find. It looked in need of some attention. The paint was flaking off the window frames and weeds were growing around the doorway.

Amy took a deep breath. "I'll be as quick as I can," she assured Lou as she stepped out of the car.

Amy rang the front door bell, and waited. There was no reply. She rang again. She could see Lou watching her, and she shrugged. Still no one came to the door. Amy decided to give up, and was walking back towards the car when she saw a girl hurrying towards the house, carrying several bags of shopping. She could only be a few years older than Amy herself – eighteen, at most. She stared at Amy suspiciously, taking keys from her bag.

As she headed for the door, Amy turned and approached her. "Hi," she said nervously. "I'm looking for Ryan Bailey. Does he live here?"

The girl inserted a key in the lock and glanced quickly at Amy. "Why?" she asked warily. "Who are you?"

"My name's Amy. I've come to talk to him about Gallant Prince."

"Well, if you're from the papers, I have nothing to say," said the girl.

"I'm not," Amy said patiently. "I'm trying to help Prince. He's had a tough time. I guess Ryan's been through a lot too." She smiled warmly, and saw a flicker of trust appear in the girl's eyes.

"So where *are* you from?" the girl asked.

"A farm called Heartland," Amy told her. "We work with horses that are injured or difficult – like Prince."

The girl looked more interested. "Well," she said, after a pause. "I'm Beth, Ryan's wife. You'd better come in." She pushed open the door and jerked her head to invite Amy in.

Amy followed her down the hall into a sitting room.

"Please sit down," said Beth, clearing away a newspaper from an otherwise spotless room. Amy sat on the sofa, and Beth sat opposite her in a wooden rocking chair.

"So how much do you know about what happened to Ryan?" Beth began, fixing Amy with a curious gaze.

"Not much," Amy confessed. "I spoke to Sam — one of the stable lads at Brookland Ridge. He gave me the address."

"Sam? How is he?" Beth asked.

"You know him?" said Amy, surprised.

Beth nodded. "I used to work there myself. So what did he tell you?"

"Well — just that Ryan was burned quite badly in the fire," said Amy. "That he's blind, in one eye. That he lost his job. And that he was really close to Prince."

Beth shrugged, and nodded. "That's all true," she said. "So — what do you want?"

"Well," Amy took a deep breath. "I was hoping I could talk to him. About Prince. The horse is totally unmanageable and we just can't seem to reach him. I thought perhaps Ryan could help."

Beth stared at Amy, and said nothing.

"Is Ryan here?" Amy asked uncertainly.

"He's upstairs," sighed Beth. "But he won't see you. Or anyone for that matter."

"Why not?" Amy persisted gently.

Beth took a deep breath. "He's just shut himself away," she

said. "I gave up my job at the stables to look after him but..."
she trailed off, her voice quavering. "Things have changed a
lot. We were only married last summer. Everything was just
great, you know? We were really happy. Then — then — the
fire happened..." Her voice broke again, and she paused.
"The horses used to be everything to him, but now he can't
do anything. I'm working at the supermarket to make ends
meet, but Ryan..."

She stopped, and met Amy's gaze with tears in her eyes.
Amy felt a rush of sympathy for her. Beth wasn't much older
than she was, but she was already having to deal with so
much — carry so much pain and responsibility.

"I'm so sorry," Amy said quietly.

"I just wish..." Beth said, blinking back her tears. "I just
wish I could get through to him. It's like I've lost him — like
he's just not there any more."

"But — he's recovered from his injuries?" Amy asked.

"More or less," said Beth. "He's lost the sight in one eye,
but he can still see fine with the other. His burns are pretty
much healed. That's not the real problem any more."

Amy hesitated. "Do you think I could speak to him?"

Beth looked doubtful. "You know, he really won't..." she
began, and stared into the distance. Amy waited. "Well,"
Beth said eventually. "I guess you can try."

Chapter Six

Beth made a mug of coffee to take up to Ryan, then Amy followed her upstairs. Beth knocked softly on one of the doors. "Ryan?" she called.

There was no answer.

"Ryan," Beth repeated. "There's someone here to see you."

There was still no answer. Amy stepped forward and put her hand on the door handle.

"May I?" she asked. Beth hesitated, and then nodded. She handed Amy the mug of coffee, and Amy opened the door.

Inside, the room was dark. The blinds were drawn, and it took Amy's eyes a couple of minutes to adjust.

"Ryan?" she said, tentatively. A hunched figure was sitting on a chair near his bed. "Ryan, my name's Amy. I've come to see you about Gallant Prince."

Ryan stared at her blankly. It was hard to make out his features, but Amy could see some scarring on the left side of his face.

"Can we open the blinds a little?" Amy asked. She moved towards the window, but before she could touch the blinds, Ryan spoke.

"Don't," he said, his voice urgent. "Don't touch them."

Amy stepped back from the window. "Oh – OK," she said. She stopped and thought for a moment. "I've brought you a coffee. Where do you want me to put it?"

Ryan didn't answer. Amy placed the mug on the chest near him, then sat on the bed. Ryan turned away from her slightly.

"I know it must be really hard for you to think about Prince, Ryan," Amy began tentatively. "You were pretty close to him, weren't you?"

Ryan shifted in his chair but said nothing.

"He's so unhappy, Ryan," Amy went on. "He's been sent to Heartland because we try to understand horses and help them through different problems. But I can't reach him. None of us can reach him. We're trying, but ... it's like he doesn't want to know."

Ryan turned his back to Amy completely. The silence hung heavy in the air. Amy hunted for anything to say.

"You know, it's weird that you're sitting here in the dark," she said, the words spilling out nervously. "For Prince, it's the other way round. It's the dark that upsets him."

She thought she saw Ryan flinch slightly at this, but it was difficult to tell in the dim light. Then he shrugged. "There's nothing worth seeing any more," he said, in a voice that was barely above a whisper.

Amy stared at him, and swallowed. "Ryan, that's not true," she said, after a pause. "There's Prince."

Ryan simply shook his head.

"I — I was wondering if you'd consider coming to see him," Amy said eventually. "I think he might respond to someone he trusts."

Ryan stared at Amy with his one good eye. "Someone he trusts?" he echoed, his voice harsh and challenging. "What makes you think Prince would respond to me?"

"I don't — I don't know anything for sure," Amy admitted. She sighed. There was another awkward pause, and Amy looked around the room as she searched for the right words. Her gaze alighted upon a pair of short riding boots, sitting neatly on the floor in the corner. A flash of hope ran through her. *He hasn't packed them away*, she said to herself. Quickly, she scanned the room to see if there was anything else. On the back of the door, half-hidden by a coat, she spotted a halter. She turned back to Ryan.

"Is that one of Prince's old halters?" she asked gently.

For an instant, Ryan dropped his guard. A look of anguish crossed his face. But then he masked it quickly.

"It's from before," he said, abruptly. He gave Amy an angry look, then turned away from her again.

"You know, Ryan, sometimes a horse can only be reached by the person who shares his pain. I know that's true. It's happened to me," she finished quietly.

Ryan shrugged. "It wouldn't help," he said coldly.

Amy opened her mouth to protest. Ryan didn't *want* to hear what she was saying.

"I won't see Prince again," Ryan said finally. "Now just go." A note of pleading had entered his voice. Amy realized there was nothing more she could do.

"Well, thanks for letting me try," sighed Amy, when she came back downstairs. Beth was chopping some vegetables at the kitchen sink, but looked up expectantly as Amy joined her. She nodded speechlessly, and Amy could see that she was close to tears again. She searched Beth's face, realizing how hard the older girl was fighting to hold everything together, and how little she had to fall back on.

"If you think of anything I can do to help…" Amy said.

Beth shook her head. "He's so determined to block out the past," she whispered. "I don't think anyone could make him face it." She put down her chopping knife and smiled sadly. "I'll show you to the door."

As she left, Amy reached out and squeezed Beth's hand, then turned and walked back to the car.

Briefly, Amy told Lou what had happened, then lapsed into silence as she thought over what she'd seen. She was filled with sadness for Ryan. It must be so hard for Beth, too, to see him buried in his world of pain. It was strange, how neither Prince nor Ryan wanted to be reached. She thought of Beth's words: *he's so determined to block out the past*. It was as though they were both stuck, unable to look either forward or back. They were locked at the same point.

"I don't know what we can do about Prince now, Lou," she said, slowly. "I was really hoping that Ryan would agree to come and help us work with him. I thought maybe he'd be able to get through to Prince, because they were together in the fire."

Lou looked at her in concern. "Isn't there anything more you can do?" she asked.

Amy sighed. "Well – it's a question of time. Eventually, perhaps..." She trailed off as Lou turned on to the freeway. "Look, thanks for taking me, Lou," she said. "I'll have a look at those bedding samples when we get back."

Lou smiled. "The bedding can wait," she said. "Prince is our priority now."

As soon as Lou and Amy reached Heartland, Amy looked for Ty. He was in Gypsy's stall on the front yard. He'd just finished grooming her and was putting the kit back into its bucket.

"So, how did it go?" he asked her. "Did you have any luck?"

"Well – I met Ryan," said Amy.

"Ryan? He's the old stable lad, right?"

Amy nodded. "He was half-blinded in the fire," she said.

"He's just shut himself away from the world. I thought it might help if he came to see Prince, but he says he won't. He doesn't want to do anything any more."

Ty frowned, thoughtfully. "Well, it sounds as though you were right to try," he said.

Amy shrugged helplessly. "How has Prince been today, anyway?"

"Pretty much the same," said Ty. "Tense, restless, snaps at me when I go anywhere near him."

"And the others?"

"Pirate's improving. The aspen seems to be having a good effect. Not so sure about Red, though. The others are kind of OK. Still a bit unsettled."

"Right." Amy nodded. "Well – I'll go and groom Sundance," she said. "He's probably feeling pretty neglected."

Ty looked at her, a strange expression in his eyes. "He wouldn't be the only one then," he said.

"What d'you mean?" asked Amy, meeting his gaze.

"Amy, we need to talk," said Ty. "About what happened. You know – us. I almost feel like you've been avoiding it."

"Avoiding it?" Amy exclaimed, feeling self-conscious. "That's not true – I just –"

"You just – what?" Ty prompted, his green eyes searching her face intently.

Amy looked away, hunting for the right words. "I haven't known what to say," she said, eventually. It was true. She'd never had to deal with anything like this before.

"But you don't need to say anything!" said Ty, stepping closer.

"Ty," said Amy hurriedly. "I just don't want anything to change."

Ty stepped back. "I see," he said, looking hurt.

Amy felt confused. "Ty! No – I didn't mean..." she started. "I just mean that I'd hate to lose you – ever. And if things change between us, I might end up losing you ... if ... if..."

"If things didn't work out," Ty finished for her.

Amy nodded. "I guess," she said uncertainly, and smiled. "Look, give me time to think about this and we'll talk some more later."

"OK," Ty said slowly, picking up the grooming kit. "I'm not going anywhere."

"Well, it's certainly absorbent," said Amy. It was Sunday morning, and Amy and Grandpa were out in the storeroom with Lou, examining the SupaDri bedding that Lou had brought back from Champions. The thick, papery flakes had soaked up over a litre of water. "And it'll be a lot less dusty than straw, which is good – some horses are allergic to straw," Amy added.

Lou looked pleased. "I'll tell them we'll go for it, then," she said. "They'll send a photographer to take some pictures of Heartland for the brochure."

"Well done, Lou," said Grandpa. "It sounds like a pretty good deal."

They headed out on to the sunlit yard, where Ty was sweeping up. "Actually, I've got something else to ask you about," said Lou. "I might as well mention it now, as we're all here."

Ty stopped sweeping and propped the broom up against the wall, looked curious.

"Go on," said Grandpa.

"I've been thinking we need some kind of weekly meeting," Lou announced, "where we sit down and talk about how all the horses are doing and anything else that's going on. Like a staff meeting."

"We all just tell each other, anyway, don't we?" said Amy, puzzled.

"Well – sort of," Lou agreed. "But with everyone getting so busy I don't think we're always very good at it. Like when I sent Swallow back to his owner before he was ready."

Amy grimaced. It had been pretty embarrassing, and dangerous, too – Swallow had been unsafe to ride on the roads, and sending him home early was nearly disastrous.

"I think that's a good idea, Lou," said Grandpa, and Ty nodded.

"It sounds a bit formal, though," said Amy.

"It wouldn't have to be," Lou said. "We could do it over supper, one evening a week. Like, Wednesday evenings or something."

"OK," Amy agreed tentatively. "Would you like me to tell Ben?"

"If you could," said Lou, hurrying off as the phone started to ring inside the farmhouse. "Thanks."

"I'll mention it to him," said Ty, picking up his broom again. "I was going to ask him to help me this afternoon. I think we should start lungeing Prince."

"*Lungeing* him?" Amy exclaimed. She thought of the struggle they'd had getting him down to the training ring only a few days before.

"He's not getting any exercise," Ty pointed out. "And we can't just turn him out with the others; he's a stallion."

"But Ty — we don't know if we can control him." She looked quickly at Grandpa, who was listening intently.

"It's going to get more and more impossible if we don't exercise him," said Ty patiently. "He's a racehorse. He's used to intensive exercise, and not getting any is making everything else ten times worse. But I was going to ask Ben to help," he added. "I think with the two of us, we should be able to cope."

Amy realized he was right. Prince was only going to get more wound up, stuck in his stall. She nodded, slowly. "Well — I guess," she said reluctantly. "What do you think, Grandpa?"

Jack looked thoughtful. "I don't like the thought of you being at risk," he said, with a worried frown. "But it does sound as though you don't have much choice."

"We'll be careful," said Ty. "I promise you that."

* * *

Later that afternoon, Amy decided to take Gypsy out for a ride on the trails. The mare had been cured of bucking, so she would soon be returning to her owners, but Amy wanted to keep riding her out alone to make sure she maintained her new good behaviour. She mounted Gypsy and set off up the track towards Clairdale Ridge.

As she passed the training ring, she was surprised to see Ty on his own with Prince on the end of a lunge-line. The stallion was trotting around, but he looked wild-eyed and resistant, his head held high. *Where's Ben?* she wondered, stopping Gypsy for a moment.

It was the wrong thing to do. The stallion immediately spotted the mare, and let out a high-pitched whinny. Gypsy jumped, and jogged on the spot. Amy tried to calm her as Ty moved quickly to shorten Gallant Prince's lunge-line and grab his bridle. But his sudden movement startled the fractious stallion. When Ty was only a stride away, Prince reared up, his hooves flashing. Ty was taken by surprise. He slipped and lost his footing as the stallion's hooves rose again above him, striking out only centimetres away from his head...

"No!" Amy gasped. She urged Gypsy to the edge of the training ring and threw herself off the mare's back, looping her reins over the fence before leaping into the training ring. Ty had managed to scramble to his feet, but, as Amy approached, Prince snaked his neck at her and screamed a piercing stallion's scream. Once more, Ty made a lunge for his bridle, and Amy moved in as fast as she could on the other side of his head. They both managed to cling on as Prince tried to rear again. It took all their strength as he ran backwards, fighting them, trying to shake them loose, while Gypsy whinnied excitedly from the fence.

Amy felt her grip loosening. Prince was too strong for them! Then, to her relief, she saw Ben out of the corner of her eye, running up the track. "Take Gypsy away!" she screamed.

Hurriedly, Ben freed Gypsy's reins and led her up to the stableyard. After further struggling, Amy and Ty at last managed to get Prince under control.

Amy suddenly noticed a patch of blood on Ty's shirt-sleeve. "Ty!" she exclaimed. "You're bleeding!"

"I think he clipped my arm with his hoof, when he reared," said Ty. "It's nothing serious. Let's get him back to his stall."

Prince was still prancing on the spot, agitated, and constantly trying to rear. "Why wasn't Ben with you?" Amy questioned.

"He helped me get him down to the ring," Ty answered. "Prince didn't seem too bad once he was trotting around, so Ben just popped back to the stableyard to fetch his gloves. I said he should wear them if he wanted to lunge Prince."

Amy nodded in agreement as they finally reached Prince's stall. Ty quickly undid the straps of his bridle and let him loose as Ben appeared at the barn door, looking mortified.

"I should never have left you with him, Ty!" he exclaimed.

"It's not your fault," said Ty.

"But I should have been wearing the gloves anyway," said Ben. "Is your arm OK?"

"You've got to put a dressing on it, Ty," Amy insisted. "Are your shots up to date?"

"Yeah, I had one last month," said Ty. "But you're right, it does need fixing. I'll come up to the farmhouse."

Together, Ty and Amy went into the kitchen and told Lou what had happened. She fetched the first aid kit, and Ty rolled up his sleeve. The cut wasn't deep but there would be bruising.

"Lou, if Grandpa finds out about this, he might make us send Prince back," Amy said, as she applied a bandage.

Lou hesitated. "We can't hide something like this from him, Amy. You can't blame him for feeling worried. He cares about you and Ty – and he hates seeing anyone put at risk. That's all."

"That's more or less what he said this morning," Ty agreed.

The three of them looked at each other, feeling dismayed. Suddenly, Amy stood up. "I don't care what Ryan may say," she said. "I know deep down that he can help Prince. I'm sure he hasn't blocked him out completely. He still has his halter hanging on his door. I have to ring him."

She fetched Ryan's number and picked up the phone.

"Beth?" said Amy when the phone was answered. "It's Amy, from Heartland. Could you ask Ryan to come to the phone?" she asked. "Please – tell him we really need his help." She quickly explained what had happened with Prince.

Amy waited patiently for Beth to come back to the phone. After what seemed like forever, she heard Beth's voice again.

"He won't come," she said. "I've begged him but he just doesn't want to know."

Amy felt her heart sink. "Is there really no way you can persuade him?" she pleaded.

"I'm sorry, Amy," said Beth, her voice breaking. "I wish he'd listen. Not just to me. To anyone."

"OK," said Amy, more gently. "Thanks for trying, Beth."

Amy sat back down at the kitchen table.

"We just have to keep on working Prince," said Ty. "There's nothing more we can do."

Lou took a deep breath. "I don't know how long we can keep going, though," she said. "Especially if Grandpa finds out."

Amy looked at her sister pleadingly. "Do we have to tell him, Lou?" she asked. "Can't we give it a few more days?"

Lou looked from Amy to Ty and back again. "Well…" she said. "OK. I won't say anything – yet. But if there's no improvement soon, we'll have to let him know."

At school the next day, Amy confided in Soraya about Ty's near miss with Prince. "I just keep seeing Prince's hooves flying towards Ty," she said, her face pale. "It was my fault, I shouldn't have taken Gypsy past the training ring. That was what triggered it. If anything serious had happened to Ty…" she trailed off.

Soraya's eyes searched Amy's, full of concern. "Amy, I know Ty's kind of special to you…"

Amy looked at her friend quickly. "It's not that, it's —" she stuttered, and stopped.

"Is there something you want to tell me?" Soraya probed.

Amy blushed slightly, her thoughts in turmoil. "No! Well — I mean — I don't really know." She looked at her friend honestly. "Promise you won't say anything to anyone."

"Of course!" breathed Soraya.

"Well, we kissed on Christmas Eve."

"Amy!" Soraya exclaimed. "How have you kept *that* quiet? I'd have been telling everyone."

Amy grinned sheepishly, then her smile faded. "Soraya, Ty's always been my friend. I'm terrified of losing him. What if things went wrong? It was bad enough losing Matt."

"Don't be dumb. You haven't lost Matt," said Soraya reassuringly.

"Oh no? When did he last hang out with us? We haven't seen him for ages — not since he's been dating Ashley."

"Well … I guess that's what happens when you're dating someone," said Soraya. "It's kind of sweet, in a way."

"*Sweet?*" said Amy in disgust. So much had changed in her life in the last year — she'd lost her mother, then Pegasus, and it was hard to take when a good friend like Matt disappeared, too. What if she and Ty ended up falling out as well? Amy felt cold inside at the very idea. But then she pulled herself together. "Anyway, promise you won't tell anyone about Ty," she finished.

Soraya nodded. "I promise, I won't say a word."

Chapter Seven

Lou made a special effort with supper on Wednesday evening. As Amy came in from the stable yard, the comforting smell of chicken pie greeted her.

"Smells great!" said Ben, coming in behind her. "Hey, maybe we should have a meeting every night if the food's going to be this good!"

Lou grinned at him. "Yeah, right," she said. "Like I'd get any work done if we did that!"

Soon, Jack, Ben, Amy and Ty were sitting at the table. Lou sat at the end with a pile of papers next to her.

"I've created a file for each horse," she said, starting to serve the pie. "We can jot down how they're getting on, then I can type up the details later. Maybe we could offer a report for owners, as part of the service. What d'you think?"

"Why not? Sounds good," said Jack, with a smile. "This is all very organized. Are the horses in any particular order?" he teased.

"Alphabetical, of course," said Lou. Then she grinned. "Only joking," she added hurriedly.

In between mouthfuls of pie, they started discussing the horses. Top of the list, of course, was Prince.

"There's not a lot we can say at this stage," Amy said honestly, shooting Ty a nervous glance. They still hadn't told Grandpa what had happened on Sunday afternoon.

"Is there any progress at all?" Jack asked.

"Well — no. Not exactly," said Amy.

"So do you think you're going to get anywhere with him or not?"

Amy thought quickly. It went against everything in her to admit defeat. She took a deep breath.

"Yes, I'm sure we can make a difference," she said firmly. "But it's still very early days."

"The problem is, he's unpredictable," said Ty. "And it's too early to say what effect the remedies are having."

Grandpa looked at everyone's solemn faces. He took a deep breath and sighed.

"Whatever we do, it's going to take time," said Amy hastily, before he could speak. "Prince is too badly damaged to be cured in just a couple of weeks."

"Amy, the issue isn't just Prince," Grandpa said quietly. "I know he's important, but you have to think of the other horses too. And your own safety. I'm aware how dangerous he is. Your mother would never have risked herself and everything else at Heartland for the sake of just one horse."

Amy's met Grandpa's gaze. She knew he was right. He smiled gently. "And we need to let Luke Norton know if we're wasting our time," he concluded.

There was a brief silence, as everyone let his words sink in. Then Lou stood up. "Seconds, anyone?" she asked, opening the oven door. The brief interruption seemed to break the heavy mood.

"Yeah, please," said Ben, giving her his plate. "This is my kind of food." Lou cut into the second pie. "At least Gypsy's doing well," Ben commented, as Lou handed his plate back to him.

"She is, isn't she?" Amy agreed. "She hasn't bucked for weeks."

"Is she ready to go, then?" asked Lou.

Ben and Amy exchanged glances, then both nodded. "I'd say so," said Ben.

"Good," said Lou. "What about Melody and Daybreak? Daybreak's doing OK, isn't she?"

"Yes," said Amy slowly. "But she's still pretty feisty. She needs a couple more weeks. I want to be sure she'll respond well to a new owner."

To Amy's surprise, Ty shook his head. "She'll always be feisty," he said. "That's just her personality. I think she's ready to go now."

"Ty!" Amy protested. "You know how difficult she was before."

"Sure," said Ty. "And I know how good she is now."

"But not all the time," Amy insisted.

They fell into silence again.

"She's always good with me when I handle her," Ben said reasonably, after a minute or two. "I haven't had any problems for a while now."

Lou looked at Amy enquiringly. Amy stared at her plate and said nothing.

"Amy," said Ty quietly. "You want to keep Daybreak because you have a bond with her. I know she's special to you. You just don't want to lose her."

"That's not true!" said Amy, but with less conviction.

"I think it is," said Ty, challenging her with his gaze. "You say you don't want anything to change," he added significantly. "Well, you know, Amy, sometimes things have to change, whether you like it or not."

Amy's cheeks flushed an angry red. She glared at Ty. The atmosphere suddenly felt very charged.

Lou turned to Ben. "Do you agree with Ty, Ben?" she asked, awkwardly. "I think I do," said Ben, looking slightly embarrassed. "They're both ready to go."

"Right," said Lou firmly. "Well, tomorrow we should start looking for a new owner for them both."

Amy sat in silence for a few minutes, avoiding everyone's gaze. She felt humiliated. She couldn't believe that Ty had disagreed with her like that, and in front of everyone else as well. Especially using the very words she'd said to him!

By the time they had finished, it was long past nine o'clock. Ben and Ty headed off, and Amy helped Lou clear away the dinner things. Then she slipped out on to the yard and went to Melody and Daybreak's stall. Melody was standing up, dozing, and barely shifted as Amy let herself quietly into the stall. Daybreak was curled up on the straw, but she instinctively scrambled to her feet at the sound of the bolt.

"Hi there," said Amy, holding out her hand to the filly. Daybreak snorted eagerly, her eyes shining brightly in the dim light of the stall. Amy knelt down and put her arms around her neck.

"I don't want you to go, baby," she whispered, feeling a lump in her throat. Daybreak nudged her curiously, and Amy stroked her tufty mane. Ty's words flashed through her mind again — *things have to change, whether you like it or not*. But who was he to say that to her? He wasn't the one who'd had his whole life turned upside down! Maybe if he had, he'd understand how difficult it was to keep losing the things she loved.

Amy's mind turned to Ryan, sitting in the darkness on his own, trying to cope with the loss of so much — his life at the stables, and, above all, Prince. She thought of his scars, and his damaged eye. She felt ashamed of herself — at least she was still fit and well. But she *had* lost a lot, and she'd had to move on. Surely she could show Ryan that whatever happened, there was always a new beginning? He needed to regain his trust in life and find something to believe in. He had to face his past, and face up to meeting Prince.

Amy's thoughts went back to Spartan. She hadn't given up on him. She'd kept on and on until he realized that it was better to trust her than stay on his own with his fear and pain. As she smoothed Daybreak's silky neck, Amy suddenly realized that she couldn't give up on Ryan, either. She kissed the filly's nose and got to her feet.

"See you in the morning, girl," she said, letting herself out. She hurried over to the back barn and made her way to Prince's stall where, as usual, he paced around restlessly. He started as she approached, snorting nervously.

Amy leaned over the half-door and fixed his rolling eyes with her gaze. "I'm not giving up on you, boy," she said to him, softly. He stood still in the middle of his stall, his muscles tense, ready to leap back. Amy stared at him, determinedly. "I'm going to bring Ryan to you if it's the last thing I do."

Amy got up early the next morning, feeling more positive than she'd felt for days. She greeted Ty with a slightly awkward smile as he walked into the yard.

"I've already fed the geldings," she told him. "I'm just about to start the feeds for the front stalls."

"I'll get on with mucking out, then," Ty said, in a slightly guarded tone. He hesitated. "Amy... I'm sorry. About last night."

Amy met his gaze. "I'm sorry, too," she said. "And Ty ...
about ... you know. Can we talk?" She smiled.

Ty looked surprised. "Well – I guess. Yeah, of course."

Amy looked at her watch. "But maybe not right now –
we've got seventeen horses to deal with."

"No," Ty grinned, obviously relieved. "Well, after school,
then."

As usual, the morning turned into a scramble to make the
bus on time. After sweeping the yard, Amy realized she had
only ten minutes to shower and change. She dashed inside
and leaped up the stairs. Nine minutes later, she was tearing
back down again.

"Lou! I'm off!" Amy called. She grabbed her coat from
where she'd left it on the back of one of the chairs.

"See you," Lou replied. Then, as Amy was halfway through
the door, she called, "Oh, Amy!"

"Lou, I gotta go!"

"Wait – there's a package for you –"

Amy stopped and stuck her head back around the door. "A
package?"

"Here – take it with you!" said Lou, hastily stuffing it into
Amy's outstretched hand.

"Open it, then!" Soraya cried, as Amy showed her the brown
package on the bus.

"I will, I will," Amy gasped. "Just hang on a minute."

"It looks like a book," said Soraya.

"No, it's too light," Amy told her. She started to tear off the layers of tape. "More like a video." She opened one end and peered inside. "Yep," she said, frowning in puzzlement. "Definitely a video."

She finished unwrapping the package and a note fell out.

Dear Amy,
I found this the other day when I was sorting out the office. Don't know if it'll help, but you might as well have it.
  Sam

"Who's Sam?" queried Soraya, who hadn't been able to resist reading over Amy's shoulder.

"The stable lad at Brookland Ridge," Amy said slowly. "The one I went to see about Ryan."

"Oh right," said Soraya. "So what's he sent you? Is there a label on it?"

Amy opened the case, but the video didn't have any details. "Nothing," she said, still feeling puzzled. "I'll just have to wait till I get home to put it on."

"All day? That's going to kill you!" Soraya teased.

Soraya was right. Amy knew she wouldn't be able to concentrate. For once even the sight of Matt and Ashley sitting together in class didn't bother her. All she could think about was what might be on that video. The moment she got home, Amy headed straight for the VCR, not even bothering to take off her coat. She slotted the video into the machine and pressed play, sitting down on the edge of an armchair to watch.

At first, she couldn't understand why Sam had sent it. It was odd races from the previous season, taped from the TV. But then, at the end of the second race, the screen went blank for a few seconds. When it resumed again, a familiar face appeared – Ryan's. Amy leaned forward expectantly.

The difference between this Ryan and the one she'd met took her breath away. On the video, his face was smooth and boyish with a deep sparkle in his dark brown eyes. He spoke confidently into the microphone, a broad smile on his face.

"He knows what he's got to do," he was saying. "He's as ready as he's ever going to be."

"Can we quote you on that?" asked the interviewer, laughing.

"Yeah, yeah, I guess," Ryan laughed.

"So that's straight from Ryan Bailey, Gallant Prince's stable lad," the interviewer announced to the camera. He turned to Ryan once more. "If you're that confident, you'll have something on the race yourself?"

For a moment, Ryan's face became serious. He shook his head. "I never gamble on Prince," he said. "You don't gamble on your friends. I just want him to come back safely to me."

The camera moved in closer, and Amy looked into Ryan's eyes. There was no mistaking the love and commitment in his words.

The video cut to the race itself. Amy imagined how Ryan must have felt, seeing Prince out there on the tracks, straining every sinew in his body to do his best. She willed the stallion to win. He did — by a full length and a half. Amy sighed as the scene changed once again, this time to the winners' enclosure, where Prince stood proudly, still looking bright-eyed and alert, barely affected by his run. Amy got out of her armchair and moved closer to the screen, scanning the busy scene for Ryan. Luke Norton was there, next to Prince, and another man she didn't recognize, but whom she guessed must be the owner. Then, at Prince's head, holding on to his bridle and praising him, Ryan appeared. As the camera panned round, Amy caught a fleeting glimpse of the stallion resting his nose under Ryan's chin and Ryan's glowing face.

Amy replayed the video — and there it was again, a moment of pure communication between Ryan and Prince. She hadn't been mistaken. The camera moved away to pan over the crowds, then the video cut to another race. Amy stared for a moment, then turned the TV off. This video held the key to it all, she was sure of it. Again, she thought of Beth's words — *he's so determined to block out the past*. She was sure he wouldn't be able to block this out — if only she could persuade him to watch it...

"Amy?" Ty's voice disturbed her thoughts.

"In here," Amy called, still staring at the blank screen.

Ty came in and looked at her, puzzled. "What are you doing?"

"Sam sent me a video," she said.

"Sam?" Ty frowned for a moment, then he clicked. "Oh yeah. The stable lad up at Brookland."

Amy nodded. "The video was of Prince. I was just watching it."

"Did it tell you anything?" Ty asked.

Amy got up. "I don't know," she said slowly. "But I've got an idea. Were you looking for me?"

"Yeah." Ty gave her a slightly awkward look. "Lou's arranged for some people to come and see Melody and Daybreak. They should be arriving pretty soon. I thought you ought to know."

"Already!" Amy cried, dismayed. She stared at Ty, all her feelings of uncertainty from the night before suddenly coming back to swamp her.

"It does seem pretty sudden," Ty admitted. "Lou did some ringing around during the day and a couple said they wanted to come right over. But she's had to go to the bank and the supermarket, so I said we'd handle it."

"Great!" snapped Amy. "Thanks a lot, Lou! I guess I ought to go get changed, then."

Chapter Eight

Once she was in her bedroom, Amy tried to calm herself down. *Melody and Daybreak have to go*, she reminded herself. *It's not going to be easy, however long it takes to find someone. Come on, Amy. Remember all the good things.* She took a deep breath and headed downstairs.

On the yard, Ty was already talking to a pleasant-looking couple in their early forties. Amy walked up to them.

"Hi, I'm Amy Fleming," she said politely.

"Pleased to meet you," said the man. "Jon Sleighman. And this is Carole, my wife."

Amy nodded and smiled. "Melody and Daybreak are in the front stalls here," she said.

She and Ty quickly put halters on the horses and led them out on to the yard.

"Pretty foal," said Jon. "Nice-looking mare, too. Hey,

girl." He stepped forward and offered Melody his hand to sniff. Carole approached Daybreak and did the same. Amy watched them carefully. They were clearly used to being around horses.

"Daybreak had some problems initially," she told them, explaining Daybreak's history. "We're handling her really carefully so that she'll trust the person who trains her, when she's old enough."

"Oh, you don't need to worry yourself about that. We weren't going to train her," laughed Carole. "Not for riding, anyway. We quit riding a few years back. We kinda want a big family farm, you know — goats and sheep, mainly. We used to have a couple of riding ponies, but we sold them when we gave up riding."

Ty and Amy exchanged glances.

"You're not going to train her?" Amy repeated.

Jon smiled reassuringly, seeing Amy's expression. "We miss having horses around the place," he explained. "So we decided to look out for any horses needing a loving home."

For a moment, Amy didn't know what to say. She looked down at Daybreak, who was nuzzling her pocket, and thought of the little foal's potential. She had her whole life ahead of her. If she went to the Sleighmans' farm, it would be like retiring her before she'd even begun, and she'd forget everything she'd learned. Quickly, Amy made up her mind. Avoiding Ty's gaze, she said gently, "You know ... Daybreak needs some training. Like I said, she has a fiery personality.

If she's left to her own devices, she'll become unmanageable pretty quickly."

"But she's the cutest little thing," Carole protested, smiling.

"She's only like this because we work with her every day," said Amy, feeling awkward. "We have a strict routine. She needs it."

Jon and Carole looked at each other. "Well…" said Jon. "We don't really want to get into all that."

Amy nodded and smiled apologetically. "In that case, I don't think Melody and Daybreak are quite right for you. I'm sorry."

Jon and Carole took in her words, looking uncertain. Amy could see their disappointment, but she was sure she'd made the right decision. She glanced at Ty, but couldn't read his expression. "We'll certainly bear you in mind if we have horses that are more suitable," Amy offered.

Carole looked pleased. "OK," she said. "We'd appreciate that." The couple patted Melody and Daybreak. "Mind if we look around before we go?"

When they had gone, Amy began to feel anxious. Ty hadn't said much during the visit. What if he thought she was just trying to stop Daybreak from going?

"So – did you think I was wrong?" she demanded, looking over the half-door into the stall where he was grooming Melody.

Ty stopped, and looked at her. "Of course I didn't," he replied. "They weren't right for Daybreak."

Amy felt relieved. She hesitated. "It was just that ... last night —"

"Amy, you know I think Daybreak's ready to go, but..." Ty trailed off, seeming to hunt for words. He fiddled with the brush in his hands.

Amy nodded. "I know she is too," she agreed. "You're right."

"But I shouldn't have said what I said," finished Ty, looking embarrassed.

Amy was surprised. She looked at him, her eyebrows raised.

Ty continued. "You know — the stuff about accepting change. That was sort of about something else. It just came out. I didn't mean it."

"I know, Ty." Amy felt suddenly nervous, and looked at him honestly. "I know what it was about. I think I just ... need some time," she said uncertainly. "It's not that —" she began, then stopped.

Ty stepped out of the stall and took her hands. "I've told you, Amy," he said, looking deep into her eyes. "There's no hurry."

Amy heard the sound of Lou's car coming up the driveway, and swallowed.

"No ... no. I'm ... glad," she said.

As Lou's car appeared in the driveway, Amy let go of his

hands hurriedly. Lou's car door slammed, and she smiled. "I'd better tell Lou how it went with the Sleighmans," she said.

Lou was disappointed with the news. "I guess I didn't ask the right questions on the phone," she said, dumping several boxes of groceries on to the kitchen table.

"We need someone who's going to work properly with Daybreak," Amy explained, taking the packets of cereal and putting them into the cupboard.

"I'll make that more clear from now on," said Lou. "What was in your package, by the way?" she asked.

"It was a video. Of Ryan and Prince, before the fire."

"Really? And is it any use?" Lou seemed puzzled.

Amy frowned thoughtfully. "It might just jolt Ryan out of himself – make him realize how badly he and Prince need each other – if only I can get him to watch it. He might not agree, but it's worth a try."

"So you'll need to make another trip?" Lou looked awkward. "I'm really busy on Saturday, Amy. I can't head up there this weekend."

"That's OK," said Amy. "I'm sure I'll find someone to take me."

When she'd finished helping Lou put everything away, Amy went back out to find Ty. He was just finishing up with Melody and was putting the grooming kit back into its box.

"Ty," she said tentatively, "You're taking Saturday off, aren't you?"

Ty nodded. These days, he hardly ever got round to taking days off; there was always too much going on at Heartland. "Yeah, why?" he asked.

Amy looked awkward. "What were you planning on doing?" she asked. "You said you were going shopping or something."

Ty looked mystified. "Yeah, during the day. Then I'm catching up with a few friends in the evening."

"Where are you going to do your shopping?" queried Amy.

"What is this? Some kind of quiz show?" asked Ty good-humouredly.

Amy smiled. "No — it's just that I want to show that video to Ryan, and Lou's busy," she explained.

Ty grinned. "Ah, I see," he said. "Well, why don't I take you? I could do my shopping in Baltimore."

"You read my mind," laughed Amy, feeling relieved. "But are you sure that's OK?"

"Course it is," said Ty. "Might even be fun," he added teasingly.

Amy nodded, and their eyes met for an instant. "That's brilliant," she said. "I'll check with Beth to make sure she's not working."

Later that evening, after supper, Amy went to the phone and punched in Ryan's number.

"Beth?" she said, when she answered the phone. "It's Amy, from Heartland."

"Amy," Beth said flatly.

Amy thought she sounded tired and depressed.

"How are you?" she asked gently.

Beth sighed, and didn't answer the question. Instead, she said, "Listen, Amy. I know you want Ryan to visit Prince, but there's nothing I can do to persuade him. There really isn't. I tried really hard last time you rang."

Amy chose her words carefully. "Beth, I understand. It must seem like he'll never change his mind. But nothing stays bad for ever."

"I'm not so sure," said Beth.

Amy could hear the doubt in her voice, and wished there was more she could say to reassure her. "I have something that might help," she said. "You told me that Ryan wants to block out the past. Well, Sam's sent me a video of one of the races that Gallant Prince won last season. It shows Ryan and Prince together like they used to be. Could I come and show it to him?"

Beth was silent for a few minutes. "I doubt he'll watch it," she said eventually. "But you're welcome to come over, if you want."

"Could I come on Saturday?" Amy asked. "Are you working?"

"Only in the morning," said Beth. "You could come in the afternoon, after two o'clock."

"Thanks," said Amy. "I'll see you then."

She put the phone down and went outside. Ben and Ty had gone home for the night, and all was quiet on the front yard. She breathed in the cool air, and walked up the track towards the turn-out paddocks. She could see a few stars where the clouds had parted in the sky, and she gazed up at them, thinking. Last night's meeting already seemed an age ago. She thought of Ty's words once more: *sometimes things have to change...* He was right. She hoped she could show Ryan how to accept the past – until he did she felt sure he wouldn't be able to face the future.

It was drizzling with rain when Ty and Amy set off towards Baltimore on Saturday. It felt odd to Amy, heading out of Heartland in Ty's pick-up – nearly all the time they spent together was on the farm, with the horses. But it felt good, too. After a while, Ty put on some music and they drove along listening to it.

As they sped along the freeway, Amy thought about the conversation they'd had after the Sleighmans' visit. She was still feeling confused – and slightly guilty.

"Ty," she said hesitantly. "You do understand, don't you?"

"Understand what?" asked Ty, glancing at her quickly.

"What I said. About ... needing some time."

Ty looked thoughtful. "I guess," he said slowly. He paused. "You're afraid things might not work out. Right?"

"Kind of," said Amy. "It's just that – I don't know what I'd do, if we weren't friends any more. You know, if…"

She didn't finish the sentence, and Ty concentrated on overtaking a truck. When they were past it, he said, "But you know, I feel exactly the same way."

"You do?" asked Amy uncertainly.

"I don't want to lose you, either, Amy. Not for anything," said Ty. He paused, then added softly, "The most important thing is that we're friends. Everything else can wait."

As they drew up outside Ryan and Beth's house, the rain started coming down more heavily. Amy pulled her coat around her and got out of the car.

"See you later," she said to Ty, making a run through the rain for the front door.

Beth opened the door almost at once. "Hi," she said, looking uneasy. "So you've brought the video."

"That's right," said Amy.

Beth opened the door wider. "Well, come in. I'll take your coat, you must be soaking."

Amy sat down in the sitting room and pulled the video out of her bag, while Beth made them both a hot drink.

"Which race is it?" called Beth. She sounded uncomfortable, and Amy wondered why.

"It's at Pimlico," said Amy. "He won by a length and a half."

Beth brought through two mugs and nodded. "I know the one," she said. "The Maryland Breeders' Cup. Ryan was just so happy after that, you know?"

"Were you there?" asked Amy.

"Sure I was there." She sat down on the seat opposite Amy. "I didn't get to go into the winners' enclosure, but I was really close so it was almost as good." Beth gave a sad smile. "Can we see it?" she smiled softly.

"Yes, but I'd really like Ryan to see it too," said Amy, trying to express her determination. "That's why I've come."

Beth shook her head, looking more uncomfortable. "It's like I said, Amy. I've told him about it," she said. "Why don't we just play it with the volume turned up a little..."

Beth looked wretched, and Amy didn't know what to say. If Beth had already asked Ryan, there was little she could do. But she *had* come a long way, and she was convinced that the video would make a difference. She wasn't going to give up so easily.

"Can I at least try talking to him again?" asked Amy determinedly.

"Well – I'll go and try again first," said Beth. She went upstairs, and Amy heard her knocking on Ryan's door and speaking in a low voice. Amy waited. There was no response, and Beth came back, looking distressed.

"It's no use," she said. "To be honest, I think he's getting worse."

"Please let me try," begged Amy.

Beth shrugged. "OK. If you want."

Amy went to the door and knocked. Ryan didn't reply.

"Ryan, I've brought something to show you," said Amy through the door. "It's a video. Of Prince, when he won at Pimlico last season. Sam gave it to me."

There was still no response. Amy stared at his door. What could she do? She couldn't *make* him watch the video. It was the same with join-up – it had to be a choice. Forcing either a horse or a person to do something never worked in the long run. In frustration, she went back and sat with Beth. Beth was sitting playing with the video box, turning it over and over in her hands.

"I'd like to watch it anyway," said Beth. "I – I'd like to see things how they were. Everything's changed so much."

Amy looked at her sympathetically. "You must miss the horses, too," she said. "Couldn't you go back and work at the training farm, once Ryan's better?"

Beth shook her head. "I can't go back there, it would make things too awkward. It doesn't matter so much for me. I'd only been there a couple of years. But for Ryan..."

"How long had he been there?" asked Amy.

"Since he was fourteen," Beth replied.

Amy nodded.

"It's good to talk about it," said Beth, giving Amy a grateful smile.

"Shall we watch the video then?" Amy asked. Beth nodded eagerly. She opened the box, and slotted the video it into the VCR.

* * *

Beth's face broke into a wistful smile as Ryan's happy, boyish face grinned into the camera. She watched the screen intently.

"All the other lads used to tease him," she told Amy. "He adored Prince like a … a … little brother."

As the camera moved in on Ryan's face, Amy heard a sudden sound. She looked around. Ryan was standing in the doorway. Beth followed Amy's gaze.

Amy felt moved as she saw the sad expression on Ryan's face. Slowly, he moved over to the sofa, his good eye never leaving the screen. Amy shifted up, and he lowered himself slowly down beside her. Beth, her face full of amazement, moved from the armchair.

"Ryan," she whispered, and squeezed on to the end of the sofa next to him.

The three watched in silence for a few more minutes, until the video reached the end of the interview. As the old Ryan spoke, Amy turned round. She felt a tug of emotion as she saw Ryan sitting quietly. Beth had put her arm around him and was rocking him gently.

"It was all my fault," he said under his breath. "If I hadn't been so stupid, he'd still be racing."

"Why?" asked Amy. "Sam said you got blamed because you were the one on duty — but I still don't see how it was all your fault."

"It wasn't," said Beth softly, but Ryan hardly seemed to hear her.

"I ruined his life," he said, his voice full of anguish.

"Ryan, wait, wait," Amy said urgently, throwing a bewildered look at Beth. "What happened?"

Ryan paused, and looked up.

Amy met his gaze. "Tell me, please," she encouraged.

Ryan hesitated, then began to speak.

"I was on late duty — it was one of the stable rules, one of us always had to stay overnight. There's a special flat, and we had a rota. It was real cold in the stalls that night, so at the start of my shift I set up three kerosene heaters. I thought they'd be fine. The horses couldn't reach them… But some of the kerosene must have leaked or something. And with the block being pretty dry, the fire spread fast."

"It wasn't just that," broke in Beth. "Someone else stacked the hay for the morning feeds right next to a heater — one of the guys who was just about to go off duty. He shouldn't have left it there; it was really dumb. But then he went off before the fire started, so Ryan took the blame."

"But it was still me who put the heaters out," insisted Ryan.

Amy listened intently. "But what happened next?" she asked. "Prince broke loose?"

"His stall was closest to where the fire started, and the heat got intense pretty fast. He broke down his door and tried to find me," Ryan said, his voice breaking up. "I'll never forget that. He was wild with pain — I can't believe I did that to him. I'll never be able to face him again."

"But wasn't it you who went into the stables and brought out the other horses?" said Amy.

"Yes, it was," Beth interjected again. "That's how he lost the sight in his eye."

"I was fetching the last horse," said Ryan. "It was Masquerade. I'd freed all the others. By the time I got to his stall, his half-door was already on fire and he was in a state, he was wild with panic. I managed to yank the door open and he just barged past me. I fell —" Ryan stopped, his throat drying up.

Beth finished the sentence for him, quietly. "On to a burning block of wood," she said.

The terrible image of the scene filled Amy with distress. She took a deep breath. "You mustn't blame yourself, Ryan," she said gently. "You did everything you could for the horses."

"But the fire *was* my fault," said Ryan. He turned to Amy. "After it happened, I was in hospital for about three weeks. When I came out, I knew there wouldn't be a job for me. How could they keep me on after what I'd done? He gulped hard. "Now it's too late. I've ruined Prince, I've ruined everything."

"You haven't ruined anything," Amy protested, desperate to reach him. "Prince needs you. I know he does. I don't think there's any more we can do unless you come and see him. Nothing's ruined, Ryan – it's just changed. Prince could have a good life at stud – but only if he can get over his fear."

Ryan shook his head vehemently. "He won't forgive me," he said, fiercely.

Suddenly, Amy felt frustrated. Ryan was still alive – and so was Prince. Why wouldn't Ryan reach out for the one thing he had left? She thought of her mother, and how much she ached to see her again. That wasn't going to happen, ever. But at least Ryan had the chance to start again.

She began to speak, the words tumbling out of her. "Ryan, Prince isn't blaming you," she said. "He's suffering. He's stuck – he can't get over what the fire did to him. He's just like you. He can't trust the world around him or the people in it. It's like he's constantly on the edge of panic."

Ryan didn't say anything, but Amy could tell he was listening. She carried on, feeling more and more determined as she spoke. "You've got to come through this together, Ryan. Prince needs someone who understands what he's been through. You can't shut yourself away here, feeling responsible for what happened. It's not fair to Beth, or you, or Prince. Don't you think you've punished yourself enough?"

Amy paused for breath, and Ryan looked at her, shame mixed with fear on his face. "If you really think it was all your fault, you *owe* it to Prince to try and help him! It's the least you can do," Amy finished passionately.

Ryan stared at the floor, and was silent. Amy waited, wondering if she'd said too much. But what else could she do? She *had* to convince him. "You know, I understand how you feel better than you think," she said, in a quieter voice. She hesitated, then added, "Last year, my mom was killed in an accident. I persuaded her to rescue an abandoned horse in a bad storm. We crashed. I — I blamed myself for what happened."

She saw Beth look at her quickly, her face full of sympathy.

"I had to face up to Spartan, the horse we rescued," Amy carried on gently. "It wasn't easy. But in the end, I realized that we needed each other. By working with him, I managed to stop blaming myself."

Ryan listened, then nodded, slowly. He studied his hands, and eventually, he spoke. "What — what does Prince look like now?" he asked.

Of course, Amy thought. *Ryan hasn't seen Prince since the night of the fire.*

"He has scars," she told him honestly. "But they're healing really well. He's unsound, and he's lost condition because he's too stressed to eat much. But we can help him through all that."

Ryan nodded slowly. "But what if…" he began, then stopped.

"What if…?" Amy prompted gently.

"What if he doesn't recognize me?" Ryan asked hoarsely, his face in his hands.

Amy stared at Ryan, suddenly realizing how hard this was for him. She hunted for the right words. "Ryan, he'll recognize you," she said. "You're still the same person. And — and — you've changed less than you think."

There was another long pause, as Ryan considered her

words. Beth took his hands, and stroked them gently. "Amy's right, Ryan," she whispered.

Ryan looked up.

"OK," he said. "I'll come."

Chapter Nine

Amy reached out and touched Ryan's hand. "It'll be hard, I know, but I'm sure it's the right thing," she said. "Really sure." She heard a pick-up draw up outside and guessed it must be Ty. "Listen, I've got to go now." She stood, feeling suddenly exhausted.

Ryan looked up from the sofa and gave an anxious smile. "I'll get the bus over to you. When should I come?" he asked.

"Whenever you like," said Amy, smiling back. "But the sooner the better."

Ryan nodded. "OK," he promised quietly.

"I'll leave the video with you," Amy said. "You might want to watch it again. And I'll leave my address too."

Amy quickly scribbled down the details of how to find Heartland and handed them to Beth who fetched her coat and saw her to the door. As Amy was about to open it, she stepped forward and hugged her impulsively. "Thank you so much, Amy," she said.

Amy smiled at the older girl. "Beth, it was you who made me realize what might help," she said. "And if Sam hadn't sent me the video—"

"No," Beth interrupted her warmly. "It was you, Amy. You believed in Ryan – you believed you could get through to him."

Amy realized she *had* believed in Ryan, because she believed that every person, like every horse, could be reached eventually. But she also recognized why. "It's like I said," she explained. "I've had to deal with a lot myself. It's taken me a long time. And you know – for Ryan, it'll be the same. It'll be tough, but at least he's trying now."

Beth nodded slowly. "I know," she said. "And thank you for helping him to start."

Amy smiled again and raced over to the pick-up.

"How did it go?" Ty asked immediately, as Amy clambered in.

"Ryan's going to come to Heartland," she said, as she fumbled for her seat-belt. Her mind flooded again with the image of Ryan's grief for Prince.

"Amy!" Ty exclaimed. "You're amazing." He studied Amy's face and saw the mix of emotions there. "I guess it wasn't easy?" he added.

"No," said Amy. "He's so ... so damaged." She suddenly felt close to tears. "Just like Prince," she added.

"Hey," Ty said gently, touching her arm.

This was too much for Amy. She buried her face in her hands.

"Hey, Amy," said Ty again, putting his arm around her shoulder. Amy leaned into it and sobbed. Then, after a couple of minutes, she pulled herself together and took a deep breath. She sat back in her seat and smiled gratefully at Ty through her tears.

"Thanks, Ty," she said, with a sniff. "It's just..."

Ty smiled. "You don't have to say anything," he said. He handed her a tissue from his pocket. Amy blew her nose.

"I guess we'd better get going," she said, more brightly. "We can't leave Ben on his own for too long."

"Sure," said Ty, starting the engine. "So when's Ryan going to come? Did he say?"

Amy shook her head. "I think we have to leave that to him," she said. "He'll come when he's ready."

Ty nodded thoughtfully as he pulled out on to the road. "Well, let's hope he comes soon," he said. "I think time's running out for our champion."

Back at Heartland, Amy checked on Ben and the horses, then headed into the farmhouse. Grandpa was just finishing a mug of coffee, and looked at Amy expectantly as she walked in.

"Guess what?" Amy said immediately, with a smile. "Ryan's agreed to come and see Prince."

Grandpa smiled. "Hey, that's good," he said. He paused. "But do you really think it will help?"

Amy's smile faded. Grandpa's enquiring look made her realize that nothing was over, yet. Ryan might have said he was coming to Heartland, but they couldn't be sure that it would make any real difference to Prince. She hesitated. "I don't know, Grandpa. But I really think they need each other," she said honestly.

Jack looked at Amy with concern. "Amy, you're a fighter. Just like your mother. Though I'm not sure even she would have gone this far." He shook his head and gazed out of the window. Then he pulled on his coat and headed for the door. "Well, I'm looking forward to meeting Ryan." He put his hand on the door handle, and looked solemnly at Amy. "If he comes."

At these words, Amy felt herself go cold inside. "I'm sure he'll come, Grandpa," she said. But a voice of doubt niggled in her head. Ryan might change his mind, and what would happen then?

Grandpa smiled. "I hope you're right, Amy," he said. "I really do."

The next morning, Ty and Amy stood at the door of Prince's stall, watching him snatch a few uneasy mouthfuls of hay from his hay net. "He's definitely getting thinner," Ty said worriedly. "He's just not eating enough."

Aware of their presence, Prince was restless, stamping a

hind hoof as though something was irritating him.

"Maybe I should try join-up again," Amy suggested.

"Is that a good idea?" Ty said doubtfully. "Wouldn't it be better to wait and see what effect seeing Ryan has?"

"We don't know when Ryan's going to show up," Amy pointed out. *If he comes.* A pang of anxiety went through her as she remembered Grandpa's words. "In the meantime, we've got to try anything we can to connect with him."

"Well ... OK," Ty agreed. "But you'll need help getting him down to the training ring. You won't be able to manage on your own."

"I know," said Amy. "Can you give me a hand?"

"Sure," Ty said. "Do you want to try now?"

Amy shrugged. "We might as well. I'll go and fetch his bridle."

She headed for the tack-room, wondering if they were wasting their time. She hoped Ryan would come quickly ... but what if he didn't? There was still the awful possibility that he might have retreated back into his shell. Who was she to think that two short visits could make such a difference?

Slinging a bridle over her shoulder, she headed back for the barn. She wouldn't allow herself to think about it. They'd have to wait and see.

"Come on, boy," she soothed, as Prince veered away from her and Ty in his stall. They drew closer, and he threw his head up. Patiently, they held their ground and tried again. After a few attempts, they managed to clip a lead-rope to his halter. Amy held on to him as Ty fought with the stallion to put on his bridle. At last, they led him, sweating and resistant, from his stall, and set off from the barn towards the turn-out paddocks.

Once he was out in the open, Prince thrashed his head around, and struck out with his foreleg. Suddenly, he stopped dead. Amy looked up at him, astonished. His ears were pricked and his nostrils flared quickly in and out. Every muscle in his body was quivering. Amy turned her head and followed his gaze.

In front of them, at the top of the track, was Ryan. He, too, was standing perfectly still, staring at Prince. He was wearing dark glasses, and his face was deathly pale. Prince craned his neck forward, still flaring his nostrils.

Ryan started to walk towards them, slowly extending his hand. "Prince?" he said in a voice that was barely above a whisper.

Prince gave a piercing whinny of recognition. He jerked the reins from Ty and Amy's hands. Taken by surprise, they let him go and he trotted forward, his neck arched and his nose stretching towards Ryan.

Ryan's face split into a huge smile. "Prince!" he exclaimed again, as the stallion reached him. Prince snorted in short, joyful bursts, nuzzling his old friend. Ryan buried his face in Prince's mane as if he wanted to convince himself this was for real.

"Prince, Prince," Amy heard Ryan say, over and over

again. Amy looked at Ty in wonder. Could it really all be as simple as this?

Chapter Ten

In a flash, Amy came to her senses. Of course Prince couldn't be transformed that quickly. She realized that his reins were hanging loose – Ryan wasn't holding on to them.

"Ryan!" she shouted urgently, rushing forward. But she was too late. Just as she reached for Prince's reins, Ty's mobile started ringing. The strident sound panicked the sensitive horse. He started violently and tossed up his head, catching Ryan unawares, butting him hard and sending him staggering backwards. Ryan's sunglasses fell to the ground and Gallant Prince reared. Amy flung herself at him, making a desperate lunge for his bridle. She missed, and the stallion plunged forward with a piercing whinny.

"No!" Amy cried, throwing herself at Prince again. This time, she caught hold of his reins. In seconds, Ty was at her side, grabbing hold of the bridle. Together, they fought to get the stallion under control.

"Prince! Prince, steady boy," Amy heard, and she suddenly realized that Ryan was with them, at Prince's head, looking into his eyes. Prince snorted, his nostrils flaring nervously, but the sound of Ryan's voice seemed to calm him down. He stopped struggling and stood, sweating, as Ryan reached and stroked his face.

"Are you OK, Ryan?" Amy asked. Ryan looked pale and shocked, but he nodded.

Amy heaved a sigh of relief. "We'd better get Prince inside," she said shakily.

Prince followed them quietly back into his stall. Amy and Ty stood outside the door as Ryan carefully took off Prince's bridle. Amy watched anxiously. Prince fidgeted and shook his head impatiently, but he didn't go crazy again. Ryan lifted the reins over his head, then stepped forward and handed Amy the bridle. He gave Ty a nervous nod, and Amy realized they hadn't been introduced.

"Ryan, this is Ty," she said. "We've both been working with Prince."

Ty smiled warmly at Ryan, and Ryan seemed to relax a little.

"Can I stay here in the stall with Prince for a while?" he asked.

Amy and Ty exchanged glances. Ty looked doubtful. "I'm not sure it's safe," he said. "What do you think, Amy?"

Amy studied the stallion. As Ryan talked to them over the half-door, Prince walked up behind him and nudged him.

Amy looked into the horse's eyes. Some of the fear and nervousness had gone, at least – but Prince still eyed Amy and Ty warily. She hesitated.

"Please," said Ryan. He turned to face Prince and stroked his neck.

"Well…." Amy hesitated. "OK. But we'll be close by, if he starts playing up. All you have to do is call."

"You've left them in the stall together?" Lou asked, looking shocked. After taking Ryan a grooming kit, Amy had hurried up to the farmhouse to tell Lou and Grandpa the news, leaving Ty to keep an eye out for Ryan.

Amy nodded. "It felt like the right thing to do," she said. "And Ty's in the barn, in case anything happens."

"But you've barely been able to handle him," Grandpa said, his face full of concern. "Do you really think it's a good idea?"

"I don't think Prince will get violent with Ryan in the stall," said Amy. "But I think it's going to be a while before he accepts anyone else." She realized the truth of her words as she spoke. Ryan's arrival was only the start – nothing was going to get better straight away. "We'll give them a little longer. Then I'll see how they're getting on."

"Well, I just hope he's safe," said Lou cautiously. "Anyway, I was just coming to find you. I've had another phone call about Melody and Daybreak. Someone wants to see them. She called me on her mobile. She's planning to drop by in the next hour."

"Oh, right. OK then," said Amy. "Well, give me a call when she arrives. I'm going back to the barn."

As Amy set foot on the yard again, she heard Ty calling her.

"What is it?" she called, breaking into a run. Ty appeared at the door of the barn, beckoning her. "Is Ryan OK?" she asked anxiously.

"Sort of," said Ty. "But I think he's finding it difficult."

Amy headed into the barn, and made for Prince's stall. She looked over the half-door. Ryan had a body brush in his hand, and was holding on to Prince's halter. Prince looked tense and awkward, and Ryan was looking frustrated.

"Come on, Prince, boy," Ryan was muttering. He caught sight of Amy watching and turned to face her. "He just won't stand still," he said. "He never used to be like this. He used to stand like a rock. He's – he's so different…" His face looked stricken.

Amy saw the doubt and confusion in Ryan's face as Prince pressed himself against the back of the stall, his body tense and unyielding.

"You can't expect him to get better at once," Amy said gently, letting herself into the stall. Prince immediately rolled the whites of his eyes and snorted warningly. Amy stood slightly behind Ryan. "You approach him," she said. Ryan extended his hand to the horse. Prince hesitated, then slowly reached out his neck. Ryan took a step forward, and Prince allowed him to stroke his mane.

Amy let out her breath. "Ryan, if you weren't here, I

wouldn't be able to stand in Prince's stall like this. It doesn't seem like much, but you *are* making a difference. Already. Believe me, it's true."

Ryan shook his head. "I thought... I thought, after what you'd said, it'd be easy," he said hoarsely. "I – I thought everything would be like it was before."

"Things are never going to be the way they were," Amy told him gently. "You have to accept that. And so must Prince. But things can move forward." She touched his arm. "We can work with Prince together," she went on. "You can already get closer to him than any of us can, and we can show you other ways of reaching him. Then, in time, other people will be able to handle him too."

Ryan looked at her doubtfully. Amy looked back, challenging his gaze. "You have to want things to change," she said. "Nothing's going to get better unless you want it to. And if you want it to, then you mustn't give up."

Amy heard Lou calling her, and guessed that Melody and Daybreak's prospective owner had arrived. "It's up to you, Ryan," she added, as she let herself out of the stall. "It's really up to you."

Amy walked round to the front yard, her thoughts whirling. She knew how hard it must be for Ryan, but she was concerned at how easily defeated he seemed. It was going to be a long haul – if he stuck at it at all. She sighed, and turned her thoughts to Melody and Daybreak.

A pick-up was parked next to the empty barn, and a woman in her fifties was talking to Lou and Ty. She smiled as Amy walked up, and held out her hand. "Jess Morgan. Nice to meet you."

"It's Ty and Amy you need to talk to," Lou was saying. "They'll tell you everything you need to know. I'll be in the farmhouse, if you need me."

Jess smiled at them. "Well, I sure remember you, but I guess you won't know me," she said. Amy and Ty looked puzzled. "I came to your open day, last October," Jess explained. "I was very impressed, and I learned a lot. Especially from that session with Lisa Stillman's Arab."

"Well, thanks." Amy smiled. She knew it was a good sign if Jess had not only come to the open day, but had been interested in their techniques, too.

"Do you work with foals a lot?" Amy asked, as they led Melody and Daybreak on to the yard.

"It's kind of becoming my speciality," Jess told her. "I run a small yard, and I have a couple of brood mares already. I've raised a handful of foals, but I'm learning all the time. You never stop doing that."

Jess gently ran her hand over Daybreak's body, then asked her to lift her feet, one at a time. "You've done a lot of the groundwork," she said, as Daybreak obliged willingly.

"Yeah. It hasn't been easy though," Amy admitted, and explained their early problems with the foal.

Jess listened intently. "Well, if you're happy for me to

take them, I'll be calling you for advice," she said. "And I'm not so far away. You can come and see how she's doing for yourself."

Amy was touched. This was exactly what she wanted to hear. "We'd love you to take them," she said, looking quickly at Ty for reassurance. He nodded. "And I'd love to visit them, too — when I have time!"

"That's settled, then," said Jess. "I won't be able to pick them up for a few days as my box is being fixed. Is that going to be a problem?"

"Not at all," said Amy. "Just give us a call."

"I will," Jess said. She shook Ty's hand firmly, and then Amy's. "I think you're doing a great job here," she added, as she headed for her car. "Losing your mom must have been really hard for you. But I'm sure she'd have been proud of you. Really proud."

No, it might not have been easy, thought Amy, as she went back to the barn to check on Ryan. *But I haven't given up. I've never given up*. As she opened the barn door, Ryan was letting himself out of Prince's stall, carrying the grooming kit. She hurried over to him, and searched his face as he handed it to her. He met her gaze frankly.

"Amy," he said. "I'm sorry about earlier. I've been thinking about what you said." He paused. "I do want things to change. You were right — Prince does need me. He doesn't understand what's happened to him, so he's lost faith in everything — just like I did. But I won't give up. I'll work with Prince until he trusts me again."

Amy felt a wave of relief wash over her. So Ryan was going to fight. "I'm glad," she said warmly. "And don't forget you won't be working alone. Ty and I will be doing everything we can to help. We won't expect you to get through this by yourself."

Ryan nodded. "I know," he said. "Thanks." He paused. "Is it OK if I come tomorrow?" he asked.

"Of course it is," Amy said. "You can come whenever you want."

"Great," Ryan smiled. "The bus journey's easy enough."

"So, did Prince calm down any more when you were grooming him?" she asked him, looking over the half-door. To her eyes, Prince was looking more relaxed than she'd ever seen him.

"A little," Ryan said. He gave a sad smile. "He used to do whatever I wanted. He's so different now. But it's good to see him," he added in a low voice. He called the stallion, and Prince came to the door of his stall.

"See you tomorrow, Mister Man," Ryan said softly, reaching up to caress the horse's face. Then he headed off up the barn. As he went, Prince turned and watched, craning his neck over the stall door. Ryan closed the barn door behind him, and the stallion gave a shrill whinny of distress.

"It's OK, boy," Amy soothed. "He'll be coming back." But Prince ignored her and stood still, staring at the barn door.

Gently Amy reached up to stroke his neck, and he flinched, then snapped at her with his teeth. Amy sighed. They were going to have to be patient. How long would it take before Prince began to accept her — or anyone else?

"You move your fingers in little circles," Amy explained. It was Thursday, and Amy had not long come home from school. Ryan had visited twice since his first arrival on Sunday, and Prince was improving steadily. As long as Ryan was there, Amy was even able to work with him herself — he would let her put on his halter and groom him as long as she didn't take too long. But he was still a long way from being really manageable. Whenever Ryan left him, he became distressed, and at night he was almost as restless as ever.

Now, Amy was standing next to Ryan, teaching him how to do T-touch. Carefully he followed her instructions. His fingers were soon moving gently and rhythmically over Prince's skin.

"That's it," said Amy, watching him closely. As he worked, she could sense that the stallion was relaxing slightly. "I'll let you carry on now, on your own," she said. "He's still quite restless with me here."

"OK," said Ryan. "I'll give it a go." He set to work, a frown of concentration developing on his face. Amy stepped back quietly and left Ryan to work with the horse on his own.

Amy hurried round to the front yard to help Ben with the

evening feeds. Ty had taken the day off, and there was a lot for just two people to do.

"How's it going with Prince now that Ryan's here?" Ben asked, as they scooped chaff, beet and alfalfa into buckets.

Amy sighed. "Slowly," she replied, shoving one of the scoops back into a feed bin and replacing its lid. "But there's definitely a difference."

"How much longer d'you think Prince is likely to stay, then?" Ben queried.

Amy looked at him quickly. Although Red had settled down thanks to the aspen remedy and lavender oil they'd been giving him, he still wasn't really himself. As far as Ben was concerned, the sooner Prince went to stud, the better — but Amy knew he wouldn't dream of saying as much directly.

"Well," she said. "Ryan is making good progress on his own. The problem is getting Prince to work with other people. That's what the owner's going to want. And that's going to take time." She frowned. "We're going to have to keep working with him while Ryan's around, then gradually build up the work we do with him when Ryan's not here. I think it's going to be several weeks before he's calm enough to go to stud."

Ben nodded. "So what will happen to Ryan once Prince has recovered?"

Amy wasn't sure what to say. She shrugged, and picked up two of the feed buckets. "I don't know, Ben," she replied, heading for the door. "It's a tough one."

"He's going to be gutted if they're separated again," Ben pointed out. "I know how I'd feel if I was separated from Red — and I haven't been through half as much."

Amy stopped and turned as the truth of Ben's words hit her. In her determination to find a breakthrough with Prince, she hadn't thought of what would happen in the long run. She'd brought Ryan and Prince back together, and now they were both facing the past, little by little. But as Prince improved, the time would rapidly approach when he would have to go to the owner's stud farm — leaving Ryan behind. Once again, Ryan would be left with nothing — no Prince, no job ... no future.

Amy swallowed. How would he cope? Had she found a cure for Prince — but at Ryan's expense?

Chapter Eleven

"I think we should keep this picture up," said Amy, pointing at the picture of her mother on Pegasus. "All the others can come down. What d'you think?" It was Saturday morning, and Amy was in the tack-room. She had asked Grandpa and Lou to come and look at her ideas for rearranging it.

"That's fine by me," said Grandpa. "I'm sure we can find room for the others around the house."

Lou nodded. "I've been checking on the prices of racks," she said. "They're not too expensive. How many do we need? Another six?"

Amy looked at the expanse of wall and nodded. "Yeah. Six should fit. That'll make a big difference."

"That's no problem. I'll order them on Monday, then," said Lou.

Ty stuck his head around the tack-room door. "Hey! It's a

bit crowded in here!" he said cheerfully. "Can you pass me Prince's bridle – oh, and that long-line."

"Prince's bridle?" Jack queried.

"Ryan's pretty much ready to start some lungeing work with him," Ty explained. "Ben and I are going to help him, though, just in case. Amy and I agreed on it last night."

"Well that's definitely progress," said Jack, looking pleased. "Has anyone told Luke Norton how things are going?"

Amy exchanged glances with Ty, and shook her head. "No," she admitted. "To be honest, I've been putting it off. I think Ryan should have as long as possible with Prince before he goes to stud. It's going to break his heart to lose him again."

Ty nodded in agreement. "It's going to be difficult."

Grandpa stroked his chin and looked thoughtful. "Well, we have to contact Luke Norton soon," he said. "We said we'd keep him posted on how we were getting on. We can't keep Prince here any longer than we absolutely need to. You know that. He's caused a lot of disruption, and things still aren't back to normal, even now he's improving."

Amy nodded, miserably. Grandpa was right. They were in a no-win situation. However they looked at it, Prince was going to have to go – and the faster he regained his trust in the world, the sooner Ryan was going to lose him.

"But we do need to give it quite a lot of careful thought," Grandpa went on understandingly. "Let's contact Luke

Norton today to say there's been an improvement, and that's all we need to say at the moment. But Ryan's going to have to come to terms with him going to stud some time soon. I can't really see any way out of that."

Amy sighed. At least they weren't going to rush into anything – and maybe something would occur to her in the meantime. "Thank you, Grandpa," she said. "I'll go and phone Luke now. And I'll get a box for the rest of the pictures."

Amy went indoors and found the number for Brookland Ridge. Quickly, she punched it in, feeling nervous.

"Hello?" she said, as someone picked up the phone. "Could I speak to Mr Norton, please? This is Amy Fleming, from Heartland."

"Speaking," said Luke Norton. "Amy. Good to hear from you. How are things?"

"Well – we have some good news," she said. "Prince has been improving steadily over the last week or so. He's much calmer, and we've started lungeing him."

"Really?" Luke sounded astonished. "Well, Mr Hartley will be pleased to hear that. He's been saying he wants to come out and see your set-up, and find out what you're up to."

"Oh – really?" said Amy, taken aback. "When was he thinking of coming?"

"Can't say exactly," Luke said. "He'll probably just drop

by when he's down your way. I'll give him the green light, shall I?"

"Yes – that would be fine," Amy stammered. "We'll be expecting him."

She put the phone down slowly, realizing she had to talk to Ryan. It wasn't fair to keep this from him – he had to face facts, and prepare himself for being parted from Prince. Quickly, she took an empty box to the tack-room and cleared the wall of pictures and rosettes, then headed up the track to see how Ty and Ryan were getting on with the lungeing.

Prince was trotting around the edge of the training ring with Ryan in the centre. His head nodded when his injured leg touched the ground, but apart from that, he looked reasonably relaxed. As she approached, Amy was struck by the change in Ryan. He looked assured and confident – a very different Ryan from the figure she'd first found hunched in a darkened room. Ty and Ben watched from the edge of the ring as the horse responded to Ryan's commands.

"He's going well," Amy said, going to stand alongside Ty.

Ty nodded. "How did it go with Luke Norton?"

Amy was about to tell him, when she realized that Ryan had overheard their words. He brought Prince to a halt and led him over.

"What's this about Luke Norton?" Ryan asked anxiously.

Amy looked at Ryan frankly. "Mr Hartley wants to come

and see how Prince is getting on, Ryan."

"Already?" he whispered.

Amy nodded. "Did you get on OK with him?" Amy asked.

"Well, I don't think he had anything against me before the fire," said Ryan. "I don't know how he felt about that." He looked at Amy miserably. "If he's coming here, I guess that means Prince'll soon be going to stud?"

Amy nodded, unhappily. "I'm sorry, Ryan. There's nothing we can do about that. Maybe Mr Hartley will let you visit," she went on, trying to think of anything that might offer some comfort. But her words sounded hollow, and she knew it.

"Maybe," Ryan nodded, leading Prince to the gate. Head bowed, he took the stallion up the track to the back barn. Ty and Amy followed him. Amy felt bad – as though everything was her fault.

"You mustn't blame yourself, Amy," Ty said softly, as if he could read her thoughts. "Ryan is so much stronger now than when you met him. You have to remember that. You can change some things, but you can't change everything."

Amy looked at him and smiled. Perhaps Ty was right.

Amy dumped her bag by the door as she came in from school. It was Wednesday – four days after she'd spoken to Luke Norton – and there had been no sign of Mr Hartley.

"Amy! Look at this!" Lou exclaimed, as Amy came in. Amy peered over Lou's shoulder.

"It's the new brochures for the Champion bedding," Lou said. "They've made a great feature of Heartland."

Amy took one and studied it briefly. "Looks good," she agreed, handing it back to Lou. She headed for the fridge.

"Is that all you've got to say?" Lou asked.

"What else is there to say?" Amy couldn't help an edge of irritation creeping into her voice. "I said I thought it looked good." She wasn't in the mood to think about brochures. She was feeling so anxious about Prince and Ryan, she could barely think about anything else.

"Thanks a lot," Lou said.

"Sorry, Lou," Amy answered, realizing she'd been a bit insensitive. "I just keep wishing Mr Hartley would show up. Then at least we'd know what was going to happen about Prince."

"Well, there's no point in worrying about it," Lou said. "He'll show up when he's ready."

Amy opened her mouth to speak, then shut it again. She and Lou had been getting on really well recently and she didn't want to spoil it.

"Have you heard from Jess Morgan?" she asked, changing the subject. "She said she was going to let us know about collecting Melody and Daybreak."

"Oh yes. I was going to tell you," said Lou, brightening. "She's coming tomorrow. I said you'd want to be here when they go, so she's coming late afternoon." Lou smiled.

"OK," said Amy, feeling a little sad. "I guess that means I should do a final session with Daybreak tonight, then."

Amy changed her usual routine with Daybreak and led her up the track towards the turn-out paddocks for a last tour of the farm. Daybreak, as usual, was curious about everything they passed, and Amy allowed her to investigate an old tractor tyre and a pile of straw covered in tarpaulin. She brought the filly back to the front yard and began to do T-touch circles along her back, whispering to her as she did so.

"You'll love your new home, Daybreak," she told her. "You've got a great life ahead of you."

Suddenly, Amy became aware of someone watching her, and she looked up. It was Ryan, studying her rhythmic movements as she worked her way up Daybreak's neck.

Amy smiled. "She's leaving tomorrow," she explained to Ryan. "I'm giving her a final treat."

"Looks like you feel pretty close to her," Ryan said.

Amy looked at him in surprise. She hadn't realized it was so obvious. She nodded, feeling a lump in her throat. "Yeah," she acknowledged. "It's going to be hard to see her go."

"Well," said Ryan. "I guess I'll be going through the same thing myself before long." He smiled bravely. "You've shown me a lot, Amy. If it hadn't been for you, I'd still be stuck in my room. I'm going to make the most of the time I have with Prince, while I still can."

Amy felt moved by his words. Ryan's situation was much, much harder than hers – she still had Heartland, Grandpa, Lou, Ty, and all the other horses. She admired his courage. "What do you think you'll do when he's gone?" she asked.

Ryan shrugged. "The doctors say I can work again. My left eye's as good as it'll ever be," he said. "So I guess I'll have to start looking for something to do. I'd like to find something with horses," he added wistfully. "But that's a bit of a long shot."

Amy finished working on Daybreak and led her back to her stall. She wished they could offer Ryan work, but Heartland couldn't afford another stable-hand. "I'm sure you'll find something, Ryan," she said warmly.

"Yeah, well, we'll see," he said. "Anyway – I'm going to lunge Prince while there's still some daylight."

As Amy settled Daybreak back into her stall, she heard the sound of a car engine coming up the drive. For a moment, she wondered if it was Jess, collecting Melody and Daybreak a day early. But when it appeared, she realized she'd never seen the car before. She stared at it. She didn't know many people who could afford a Lexus. It must be Mr Hartley.

Amy hurried forward to greet the man who was getting out of the car. He looked strangely familiar, and Amy suddenly realized where she'd seen him before – on the video of Prince's win last season.

"Mr Hartley?" she said, extending her hand. "I'm Amy Fleming."

"Pleased to meet you, Amy," said the man. "Call me Dan."

"This is my sister, Lou," Amy added as Lou appeared from the farmhouse. "She's the one who contacted Brookland Ridge." Dan Hartley stepped forward and shook her hand. "Good to meet you at last," he said.

"Have you come to see Gallant Prince?" Lou asked.

Dan Hartley nodded. "That's right. How's he doing?"

"Pretty well," Amy said. "I'll take you to see him."

"I'll find Grandpa and Ty," Lou offered.

Amy nodded. She remembered that Ryan had said he was going to lunge Prince. "We'll be down at the training ring," she called over her shoulder, leading the way down the track. Ahead, she could see Prince, trotting around the ring. Despite his characteristic nod, his neck was arched, and his stride looked free and flowing.

"There he is," she said.

Dan Hartley hurried forward, staring at Prince in amazement. "He looks almost like his old self!" he exclaimed, as he reached the edge of the ring. Amy wished she could warn Ryan, but Ryan had already spotted Dan Hartley, and he slowed Prince to a walk, looking anxious.

"Who's that working with him?" asked Dan Hartley, looking puzzled. "He looks familiar."

"It's Ryan Bailey," said Amy nervously. "His old stable lad."

"Ryan!" exclaimed Dan Hartley. "So it is. I barely recognized him. The poor guy must have taken the brunt of the flames. I didn't realize — I was just told that he'd left the training farm."

"He did," Amy admitted.

"So what's he doing here?" asked Dan.

"I tracked him down," Amy confessed. "We were having real problems with Prince. He was too locked in his memories of the accident. We realized that only someone who really understood what he'd been through would be able to reach him, so we managed to find Ryan and ask him to come and help us."

She paused as Ryan brought Prince to a perfect square halt, then carried on quickly. "Ryan's really speeded up our work. Prince might have got over his trauma eventually, but we wouldn't have been able to keep him here for that long. Only Ryan could have reached him this fast." She hesitated, then added, in a low voice. "And only Prince has been able to reach Ryan."

Dan Hartley listened to her words, stroking his chin. "Well," he said, shaking his head. "This is amazing. I never expected to see this kind of change. To be honest, I thought we'd lost Prince for good."

Amy smiled. "No horse is ever lost for good," she said, with feeling. "But there's still a long way to go. We need to make sure that Prince learns to trust other people again. If he'll only work with Ryan, that's no help to you, is it? But we're getting there," she finished, as Grandpa, Ty and Lou joined them.

Dan Hartley looked thoughtful. He leaned on the fence and watched intently as Ryan sent Prince around the ring again on the other rein. Then, to Amy's surprise, he beckoned to Ryan. Ryan halted Prince again, and walked over to the fence, carefully gathering in the long-line as he did so.

"You remember me, Ryan?" asked Dan Hartley.

"Of course, Mr Hartley," Ryan said politely.

"You've been doing an amazing job with Prince," said Dan Hartley. "I didn't think he'd make it through. But he has – and Amy tells me it wouldn't have been possible without you."

Ryan looked surprised. "I don't know about that, sir," he said, embarrassed. "Amy persuaded me to come here. I didn't think I could face Prince again. But I'm glad I did. He seems to be nearly his old self again."

Dan Hartley listened to Ryan's words, and shook his head. "Well, it's clear to me that you've had a big effect. I don't know how to thank you."

"You don't need to thank me, sir. It's been enough, seeing Prince recover."

"And would it make you happy to see him move on to better things?" Dan Hartley said, studying Ryan's face.

Ryan looked nonplussed. "Well, yes, but..." He trailed off, looking puzzled.

Dan Hartley smiled. "We need you at the stud farm with Prince. Would you consider coming to work there?"

Ryan looked at him, stunned.

"When Prince is ready, that is," Mr Hartley added. "I

know he still needs more time here first. But he'll always need someone to look after him. I seem to remember you've got a wife, haven't you? Well, you could live nearby — there are a couple of houses on the farm. We could arrange for you to have one of them."

Ryan's face split into a huge grin. He extended his hand to Dan Hartley. "That's a very generous offer, sir," he said. "I'd be proud to look after Prince for you."

Dan Hartley rubbed his hands together. "That's settled, then," he said, and looked round expectantly at Ty and Grandpa. Quickly, Amy introduced everyone, and they all began walking back up the track towards the farmhouse.

Grandpa walked next to Amy and put his arm around her. "You were right to keep trying, Amy," he said in a low voice. "Things work out for people who believe they can. I think you've shown Ryan that — and the rest of us, too."

Amy stopped and waited for Ryan to bring Prince alongside them. Ryan was still shaking his head in disbelief. "I never expected anything like this could happen again," he told them. "I thought everything was over for me."

Amy grinned, and reached up to stroke Prince's neck. *No*, she thought. *Everything's just about to begin*.

"I'll go and get Melody's rugs," said Ty the next evening, as Jess Morgan stood talking to Lou and Grandpa in the yard. She'd arrived with her horsebox about an hour after Amy had got home from school.

"OK," said Amy. "I'll be in their stall."

She headed off and stood for a moment, looking over the door at Melody pulling hay from her hay net. "Time to go, girls," she said softly.

She let herself in, and Ty appeared with travelling rugs. They led the pair out, and started buckling travelling boots on to Melody's legs. Jess Morgan came over and helped them check everything, then took Melody's lead-rope from Ty.

"Up we go," she said, leading Melody towards the ramp. Melody looked at it fearfully, and Amy remembered that she'd always been nervous about travelling. Amy stepped forward and stroked her neck as Jess talked to her in a calm, soothing voice, reassuring her. "Goodbye, Melody," Amy whispered. "Go on, girl. You can do it." She smiled at Jess as, after a few nervous snorts, Melody followed her up the ramp.

Then it was Daybreak's turn. Amy knelt quickly at the filly's side and hugged her. Daybreak nudged Amy with her muzzle.

"Goodbye, Daybreak," Amy whispered, tears blurring her eyes. With a final kiss on the filly's soft nose, Amy blinked back her tears and stood up, handing Jess her lead-rope. There would be more Melodys and more Daybreaks – mares needing help through their pain, foals needing guidance and encouragement – but none of them would touch her heart quite like this little filly. As she stepped back, Amy knew she was saying goodbye to another part of her family.

Jess showed Daybreak the ramp, and Daybreak sniffed at it curiously. Then she stepped on to it willingly to join her mother. Amy took one last look inside the box. Daybreak turned and regarded her with her bright, inquisitive eyes. With a gentle whicker the filly seemed to say goodbye as Jess slowly lifted the ramp.

Grandpa came and held Amy's hand as Ty helped Jess slot the final bolts into place. Lou stepped forward and took Grandpa's other hand.

"Goodbye – and thank you for giving me two wonderful horses," Jess said.

Amy smiled as Jess climbed up into the horsebox. "That's what we're here for," she said. "To find new beginnings for horses – and new friends, too. We'll be seeing you. I promise I'll come to see Daybreak and Melody soon."

Jess nodded as she started the horsebox. Amy waved and smiled, her heart filling with happiness as she realized that Daybreak would still be out there ... and that in her place at Heartland, there would soon be another horse – a horse who needed her, and whose life would be changed for the better.

Read the first book about

Heartland™

book one

Coming Home

"It's the stallion!" Amy called, motioning frantically to Soraya. She tugged the door further open, bumping it heavily along the ground. Once the door was open far enough to let in some light, she could see the stallion clearly – and he could see her. His eyes rolled in fear as he stood at the back of the barn, his muscles bunched and tense, his shoulders and flanks quivering.

"It's OK," Amy said to him as soothingly as she could. "I won't hurt you." Her eyes swept round the shed. The floor was bare and there was no water or food. However, the stallion's physical condition was good which meant he couldn't have been shut in for more than a day or two.

The horse called out shrilly. Amy's mind raced. If she opened the door further he might try and break free. That could be disastrous – he would either escape on to the wilds of Clairdale Ridge or end up on the narrow road. But they had to help him somehow. She swung round to Soraya. "We've got to do something!"

Soraya had her own problems. Excited by the stallion's whinnies, Sundance and Jasmine were whirling round. Sundance tried to bite Jasmine, causing the mare to rear backwards. Soraya only just managed to keep her seat.

Amy looked up at the dark sky. It had begun to rain heavily. Large drops were splashing down. Her heart pounding, she turned again to the barn and started squeezing through the gap in the door.

"Easy, now," she called to the frightened stallion. He half reared and she jumped back. "Steady!" But the horse wouldn't be calmed. He kicked out, his back hooves crashing against the barn wall.

"Amy!" Soraya called from outside. "I can't hold on to Sundance much longer!"

Amy hesitated. She knew Soraya needed help, but what about the horse? The rain was pelting down now, bouncing off the roof and forming puddles on the ground. Her mind was in a whirl. Even if she could get near the stallion how was she going to get him back to Heartland without a halter or bridle?

"Amy!" Soraya's voice was higher, more desperate, now.

Amy made up her mind. She squeezed back out of the shed and dragged the door shut. "I'm sorry!" she whispered through the crack, as she rammed the bolts home. "But I'll be back soon."

The stallion cried out frantically as he found himself in the dark again. Trying to shut out the sound, Amy turned away. Sundance had reared up and Soraya was struggling to hold on to him.

Amy raced over to her friend. She grabbed his reins and pulled him down. "Quick! We've got to get help!" Steadying Sundance, Amy swung herself up into the saddle and the two girls set off down the trail at a gallop.

By the time they got back to Heartland Amy and Soraya were soaked to the skin, their jodhpurs clinging to their legs and their T-shirts plastered against their bodies.

They clattered into the yard at a tremendous pace that brought Marion Fleming hurrying out of the tack-room. "What on earth are you doing?" She looked at Amy's wide eyes and pale face and her tone changed. "What's happened?" she asked anxiously.

"The Mallens' horse!" Amy gasped, sliding off Sundance. "They've gone, but it's shut up in a barn outside their house. Mom! You've got to help!"

"It's been abandoned?" Marion said.

Amy nodded. "We've got to go and get it!"

Marion looked at the rain pouring down around them. "We can't take the trailer out in this, Amy! The roads up on Clairdale Ridge are so steep and narrow. It would be too dangerous."

Amy pushed away the picture of the forbidding tunnel of trees high up on the ridge. "But we can't leave that horse shut in for another night!" she cried. "It hasn't got food or water or anything!"

"Nothing?" Marion said quickly.

Amy shook her head. "It's terrified, Mom! If a storm starts it might try and break free!"

Marion made up her mind. "OK, we'll go get it," she said decisively. Her voice became brisk and efficient. "You put the ponies away and get a bucket of food for the stallion. I'll get the trailer out." She hurried off. "See you in a minute."

"Here!" Soraya said, reaching to take Sundance's reins off Amy. "Go now. I'll put Sundance and Jasmine away. I'd better not come with you. Dad will be here to pick me up soon." Amy hesitated for a moment. "Go on!" Soraya urged. "You can call me tonight and tell me what happens."

"OK! Thanks!" Amy gasped. Turning, she ran after her mom.

As they drove out of Heartland the weather seemed to get even worse. The sky was heavy and dark grey. The windscreen wipers squeaked rhythmically back and forth, barely making a break in the sheeting rain. The tyres splashed noisily through the water on the road.

Amy shivered in her damp clothes. "Why do you think the Mallens left him, Mom?"

Marion shook her head, her eyes glued to the road. "I guess he might have been stolen, and then before they'd found someone to sell him off to they got scared. Maybe the police had been asking around."

"I can't believe they could just abandon him like that!" Amy exclaimed. "He could have starved to death."

Marion looked grim as she turned the trailer up the steep, winding road that led up Clairdale Ridge. "People like the Mallens don't care about things like that." The gearbox clunked as she changed down a gear to negotiate the sharp bends. Water was running in streams down the road.

They headed into the gloomy tunnel of trees. The truck and trailer crawled round the tight bends. A branch cracked loudly and thudded on to the roof. Amy jumped. She didn't like this dark passageway one bit. A tree creaked alarmingly as they passed. Amy gripped the seat and concentrated on rescuing the horse.

At last they emerged into the open. "I can hardly see a thing," Marion said, as heavy rain hit the windscreen again.

Amy peered through the blur, searching the track that led up to the farmhouse. "There! There's the turn. Not far now, Mom."

The truck splashed along the rutted driveway. Marion stopped it outside the house and jumped out, leaving the headlights on to illuminate their way. Amy grabbed the halter and lead-rope from the seat beside her while Marion put the trailer ramp down. "Which building is it?" she called to Amy.

"That one!" Amy shouted, raising her voice above the wind.

They staggered through the rain to the barn. After Marion had pulled back the bolts, they heaved the door open together so it stood slightly ajar. Amy looked in. The bay stallion stared at them, head up, nostrils flaring, eyes wild. Marion looked at him for a moment and then turned her back to the wind and took out a small container from her pocket. From inside, she took a pinch of dark, gritty dust and rubbed it into her hands. "Stand back a bit," she said softly to Amy.

Amy did as she was told and Marion squeezed through the gap in the door. The horse moved uneasily on the spot, his ears back. Turning herself sideways on to him, Marion looked at the floor. The stallion regarded her warily. Very slowly she held out her hand. The bay made to jerk his head back but then he seemed to suddenly catch the scent of the powder. His nostrils flared and he inhaled, his ears suddenly pricking up.

Amy held her breath. The powder was made from chestnut trimmings which were insensitive, horny growths found on the inside of horses' front legs. An old horseman had once taught Marion that the scent would calm nervous and frightened horses. Now, sheltering in the doorway, Amy watched to see what would happen.

Very cautiously, the horse stretched out his head. Marion stayed absolutely still, eyes averted. *I am no threat*, her body language seemed to be saying. The horse took a step forward, all the time breathing in. His delicate muzzle touched Marion's hand, his nostrils dilating. He took another step forward and lifted his head to her hair, breathing in and then out.

Very slowly, Amy saw her mom turn, and as the stallion breathed in again the fear left his eyes. His muscles relaxed and he lowered his head to nuzzle Marion's hand. She stroked him. "Pass me the halter," she said quietly to Amy.

Without the slightest objection, the horse let Marion slip on the halter. She patted him. "Come on, boy, let's get you into the trailer."

Amy heaved the door open. The horse obediently followed Marion out into the sheeting rain. Amy patted him and he nuzzled her arm. Now his initial fear was gone he seemed friendly, even affectionate.

When they reached the trailer she stood on the ramp and rattled a feed bucket. The horse stretched out his head and neck and gobbled a mouthful. Then, with no more prompting, he walked calmly into the box. Amy put down the bucket to let him eat and then, leaving her mom to tie him up, she slipped out of the side door to pull up the ramp. Her wet fingers slipped as she fastened the bolts. The wind and rain lashed down. At last Marion emerged. "Home," she said, coming round to check the bolts. "And fast."

Their faces were streaming with water as they climbed back into the truck. Marion turned the key and the engine spluttered into life. Amy shivered and squeezed water from her hair. Marion turned on the heater. It roared noisily, competing with the sound of the rain. They could hear the stallion move uneasily in the back as the rain battered the roof of the trailer.

Outside there was an ominous rumbling. Seconds later, a jagged fork of lightning split the sky and the rain started to sheet down with a new intensity. As they turned on to the steep road downwards, a crash of thunder broke over them.

The horse began to panic. His feet thudded against the side of the box, causing it to rock alarmingly. Amy glanced anxiously at her mother. The truck was gathering speed as it headed down the hill. Marion was concentrating hard, braking slowly and steadily to keep the trailer under control on the wet road.

"This is insane," muttered Marion. "I should never have let you talk me into this, Amy." Her eyes showed her anxiety as she gripped the steering wheel tightly.

Amy jumped as lightning forked straight down through the sky accompanied by an immense clap of thunder. The stallion's hooves crashed into the walls of the trailer again and again as he struggled to escape from his moving prison.

The tunnel of dark trees loomed up ahead. As they entered, branches closed over the top of the trailer, banging and scraping against it. Every muscle in Amy's body was tense. Her heart was pounding. Her breath was short in her throat.

The trees on each side of them swayed as the unrelenting wind and rain bent them against their will. The road seemed pitch-black beneath the tree canopy. Then there was a brilliant flash of lightning and a clap of thunder so loud it sounded as if a cannon had gone off overhead. Amy screamed and jumped. The horse let out a shriek as a cracking noise echoed through the tunnel.

Straight in front of them, a tree started to fall.

Marion braked violently but the tyres failed to grip the flooded surface. The truck skidded down the road, straight into the path of the tree.

Time slowed down. Powerless to do anything, Amy watched as the tree fell in horrifyingly slow motion towards them. For one wild moment she thought they were just going to get past, but then with a final creaking, crashing noise, the tree collapsed.

With startling clarity, in a single second that seemed to last for ever, Amy saw every little detail, every vein of every green, damp leaf. "*Mom!*" she screamed.

There was a bang, a sickening feeling of falling, and then nothing.

Read all the books about Heartland:

www.scholastic.co.uk/zone